Wish upon

For my mother,
the original Guardian of Memory.

And my father,
Emperor of Trivia,
who has train routes and schedules from 1936
engraved in his memory.

SARAH FITZGERALD HOBEL

Wish upon

Bibliografische Information der Deutschen Nationalbibliothek:
Die Deutsche Nationalbibliothek verzeichnet diese Publikation
in der Deutschen Nationalbibliografie; detaillierte bibliografische
Daten sind im Internet über http://dnb.dnb.de abrufbar.

© 2020 Sarah Fitzgerald Hobel
Satz, Umschlaggestaltung, Herstellung und Verlag:
BoD - Books on Demand, Norderstedt

ISBN: 978-3-7494-0494-0

Chapter 1

Lucia had thought earlier that day their nightly walk would have to be cancelled. Even though Sparky stayed by the door like a furry doorstop, it was still snowing heavily at 5:00. But then it tapered off to a few random flakes and after a supper of potatoes and sausage for herself and Sparky, Lucia started the long process of getting dressed for the walk and Sparky pranced by the door, his tongue lolling and his eyes sparkling. "I know, boy," Lucia scratched her behind Sparky's floppy ears. "It's going to be an especially beautiful night."

Lucia and Sparky lived in a snug little cabin nestled in the mountains above Zermatt. Lucia couldn`t see the village from her house so it was easy for her to pretend that she was alone with Sparky at the end of the world. The cabin was neat and functional. The living room served as the dining room and was warmed by a fireplace. Lucia´s person and belongings smelled of soot. She did her cooking on a wood stove blackened with years of fires. Her bedroom was in the back of the cabin, the only room with a door. She had an outhouse a discreet few yards away and a hole in the kitchen floor covered with a trap door where she kept milk and butter.

Her seventy-six years made her slow as she dressed, and she had so many layers of clothing that it took her twenty minutes to put everything on. The temperature in the mountains surrounding Zermatt was as frigid as if outer space had dipped down to touch the earth. Cold was her third companion on those nights, along with her dog and her memories. Sparky, a golden retriever mix, made her feel warmer. Sparky and snow pants, regular pants and stockings and three pairs of socks kept her body insulated. Rubber boots that reached her knees. Reinforced. Waterproofed. With a tattered string at the top to tighten them snug to her leg and keep the snow out.

Sparky loved these walks as much as Lucia did and knew they depended on the weather. He knew just by sniffing the air each afternoon what weather the wind would deliver in the evening. When it wasn't snowing, he stood by the door all evening, wagging his tail. During blizzards Lucia would make a fire and Sparky would curl up next to it on the floor, not even giving the door a second glance. When it was snowing the sky glowed pink-purple and walking was too difficult for Lucia. Fresh snow was the hardest to walk through. Sometimes the snow drifts piled up to her belly button and she walked more with her hips than with her feet.

After Lucia had finished dressing, they ventured outside. They took the route going away from the village, deeper into the mountains, which glowed in the moonlight. Sparky bounded away like a rabbit, delighting in the new fallen snow flying everywhere like powder. Lucia trudged behind him, admiring his energy. Such nights brought out the puppy in Sparky. The moonlight sparkled on the snow like dark secret diamonds, gems only known to the nightwalkers. Sparky bounded back to his mistress, cocked his head, indicating that Lucia should scratch between ears and leapt away again, biting the flying snow. He seemed to be laughing. Lucia stopped, lifting her chin so the moonlight shone full on her face. She had seen people do this with sunlight—skiers eating their lunches at the restaurants, hikers who have stopped for a rest. The constellations glimmered in the light of the half moon. Lucia knew the winter constellations by heart—Hydra—the serpent slithering over the mountain, Bootes—half-hidden as if his boot had gotten stuck in the snow. Andromeda galloping into the sky. Lucia smiled at Sparky cavorting in the snow under Hydra's watchful eyes. She felt a rush of love for him. She had always owned dogs, and she knew Sparky would be the last of her four-legged companions. Sparky had helped to fill her days with love. She had outlived her relatives and her neighbors, now she was alone with her dog at the end of the world, waiting for the end of her life.

Just then Sparky stopped short and howled...long and low. Long ago, there had been wolves in the mountains. They used to howl that way. Sparky had been living with Lucia for 10 years and had never made a sound like that before. "Sparky? What's wrong, boy?" The dog had frozen in place, his smile gone, his snout pointing at the sky behind Lucia. Strange, she tasted metal in her mouth. Lucia turned around to see what Sparky was looking at.

The night was absolutely silent, except for the

sound of frying bacon. Bacon? Lucia cocked her head like Sparky sometimes did when he was listening hard. It sounded like static in distance—the way her radio sounded during a blizzard. Getting louder. Lucia leaned in the direction of the noise, squinting to locate the source. Her eyes widened as she realized the sun was coming up. The sky was getting lighter behind the mountain. She glanced at her watch. 8:23. And that was p.m. Was it still thick of the evening or had her watch and time itself stopped? And since when did the sun rise in the north?

But there it was except it was the wrong color: Gold mixed with silver and getting bigger instead of rising. The sizzling sound became thunderous. Sparky howled again but it was lost in the noise. Lucia covered her ears with her hands but kept her gaze locked on the object. No, it wasn't getting bigger.

It was getting closer.

Rushing straight towards them.

The ball of light flew faster than she could think. She didn't have time to feel terror. Everything was drowned out by the light and a series of explosions like the gunshots used to cause avalanches, but louder and lower in pitch. Lucia both heard and felt them vibrating through her body. The blade of light cut the sky open over her head, she screamed but the noise was stolen out of her mouth. Silver spark fireworks rained down. The ball of light continued flying behind a rock outcropping. A brilliant flash blinded Lucia, and then an explosion knocked her off her feet. She lay there for a few seconds, dazed, an old woman lying helplessly in a snowdrift, not comprehending what had happened.

Sparky bounded over and started to lick her face. Lucia groaned and pushed Sparky gently to the side. She struggled to her feet and swayed. She didn't know if she should run away or run toward. She had lost one of her boots and the other was filled with snow. Whatever it was had literally knocked her out of her shoes. Snow had also gotten down the back of her coat and was starting to melt.

As she felt around for her boot, dark spots still streaming across her vision, she remembered that her Uncle Bruno had once told her that she could wish on shooting stars. Well, I certainly earned myself a mountain of a wish tonight, she thought.

She yanked her wet boot over her foot and stumbled in the direction of the explosion. Sparky circled her, yipping. She peered over the top of the rock outcropping. There it was, steaming and glowing, spitting and hissing. Still blistering from its ride through the atmosphere. The rock glowed orange but was fading as it cooled. At that moment she would have given anything to have another human being beside her, someone to nudge and say: "Would you look at that?"

"My wish, my wish." She looked at Sparky. "What shall I wish for?"

As she looked at the meteorite something tore across her heart, the way the meteorite had torn across the sky, and her entire being shook as if she, instead of the meteor, had fallen from a great height.

For a moment she was standing beside herself, as if part of her had diverged. Then the feeling was gone.

But she felt different. Lighter. Some sort of strange funnel had opened up within her, and she felt that burdens of the memories she had carried were beginning to spiral down. And it felt good—forgetting what might have been. To never think about those images again—yellow yarn. An English textbook. A frayed bit of rope. A crooked smile that broke young girl's hearts. Memories funneled down into nothingness. Lucia let them slide. She closed her eyes and smiled. Finally, she would be free. There would be no sorrow waiting behind her eyelids. She would spend her last days in peace.

That was a befitting wish.

Her face glowed in the dimming light from the meteor, the wrinkles of worry slipped away. She slid down the outcropping to where it lay, the size of her breadbox back in the cabin.

"Thank you," she said to the meteor, and rubbed it with snow until it was cool enough to take into her hands.

Chapter 2

Reginald C. Patterson sat in Dr. Nussbaum's waiting room, scrolling through his iPad. Donald Trump was smirking on the screen, leaning forward over a podium and looking predatory, as if he might gobble up his audience. Although Reginald was a red, white and blue Republican, he was no fan of the Donald. He was fed up with slander and mud-slinging, having seen more than enough mud in Vietnam and hearing the lies the politicians told to justify the invasion. He picked another rubric at random—International News, subheading Science. That sounded better than American Politics; almost anything was preferable these days.

The office phone rang. Brandy, the receptionist, picked it up. "Hello? Hello?" She hung up again and picked her pencil back up. No one must have been on the line. Reginald shrugged and resumed his foray into International Science while he waited.

Reginald favored Dr. Nussbaum to his last doctor because he measured time as Reginald himself did, in slices of minutes. If a patient's 15-minute consultation was up, Dr. Nussbaum just ejected the patient to make room for the next one, assembly-line style. Reginald appreciated the efficiency in that.

Reginald hoped the results of his CAT scan were in and could pinpoint his problem. His headaches had gotten worse lately, and the Almotriptan he had been taking for migraines seemed to have strange side effects. He had started seeing auras—around objects but mostly around people. He was certain Dr. Nussbaum would be able to explain that and adjust the dosage.

When he had first come to this office, Dr. Nussbaum had been fascinated by Reginald's eidetic memory and had asked him all sorts of questions: what he had eaten for Christmas dinner in 1973, who had he played with on the playground on July 11th, 1944 and the complete contents of his dead mother's wardrobe. The good doctor informed Reginald that he had a condition called hyperthymesia, an uncanny ability to recall details of his own personal life, and it was a condition rarely found in adults. Reginald had been half-expecting for Dr. Nussbaum to get a saw, cut open his skull and peer into his brain. Maybe the headaches had something to do with his memory. But amputation probably wouldn't help. That was a good joke. He could tell that one to Dr. Nussbaum.

He sat ramrod straight as he scrolled. Only his neck was bent. His posture was a remnant from his former career as a judge and an Army lieutenant colonel. He was well-dressed, subtle in a grey pullover and slacks. He had no patience for floral shirts and polyester he had seen other retirees wear. He dressed in long pants and pullovers even at summer's boiling point and never broke a sweat. He had sweated enough to fill the Pacific basin back in Vietnam. He refused to relocate to Florida, California or Arizona either. He was a Pennsylvania man through and through.

The phone rang again. "Look, whoever this is, I don't think it's funny!" Brandy slammed the phone down. Her gentle lavender aura was beginning to show veins of violet. Reginald shook his head. Probably kids playing a prank. None of them had any respect these days.

He had arrived for his appointment 7 minutes beforehand. He calculated that this was an appropriate length of time to be early. He glanced at the clock at the top of his tablet's screen. 8:42. 3 minutes to fill. He stopped scrolling and his fingertip hovered over a picture of an old woman. Half her face was lit up in the stark morning sun like one of those half-moon cookies Reginald had enjoyed as a child. She was standing in a doorway next to a golden retriever. She was holding a rock in her outstretched hand. She looked pleased and a bit dazed by her good fortune. The caption read: Woman discovers meteorite. Lucia Zurbriggen, of Zermatt, Switzerland, had found a rare meteorite while on an evening walk with her dog. The majestic Matterhorn rose behind her house, he recognized it from his travel book at home.

There were no wrinkles on this woman's face, or at least on the half face visible. Her cheeks were as smooth as a baby's. She looked serene as she proudly displayed her find.

The screen went black and Lucia Zurbriggen disappeared. Reginald pressed the 'home' button but nothing happened. The battery had run out.

"Mr. Patterson?" Brandy was standing in front of him. The violet streaks in her aura were ebbing back into lavender.

Reginald laid the tablet aside. He couldn't believe

it—not only had he forgotten to charge his tablet before he left home, he had lost track of time as well. Forgetting wasn't something that Reginald usually did. It made him uneasy.

"You can follow me please." She gave him a cheery smile and swished down the hall, glancing over her shoulder like a 40s pin-up girl.

As Reginald stood up he felt a tiny weight shift in his pants' pocket. It was his lucky charm, the only one he had—a piece of mountain crystal. He stroked it superstitiously as he followed Brandy down the hall. He admired her backside without any pang of sexuality whatsoever.

She ushered him into the consultation room and closed the door as she left. The room was brightly lit, designed to reveal every mole, spot and impurity on the human body. Books were lined up on a shelf: Haematologicy, Malignancies of the Blood, Sarcoma, Carcinoma. There were a couple probes and instruments placed neatly on a white table, but otherwise the room was sterile and about as cozy as the Antarctic tundra. Reginald's no-nonsense kind of room. He felt comfortable. Dr. Nussbaum would have answers for him.

True to form Dr. Nussbaum didn't keep him waiting long. The doctor nodded a greeting as he entered the room and took a seat across from Reginald. Dr. Nussbaum was a blandly handsome man with perfectly even features that discouraged small talk without saying a word. He didn't have an aura, at least none that Reginald could see.

"Well, the good news is that we've found the cause of your headaches." Dr. Nussbaum folded his hands like a church in front of him, and Reginald was reminded of a game he had played as a child: here is the church, here is the steeple, open the doors and see all the people. Would Dr. Nussbaum show him all the people?

No, he wouldn't.

Instead Dr. Nussbaum told Reginald that he had a brain tumor.

"I'm sorry that there's nothing more we can do for you here." Dr. Nussbaum shrugged his shoulders and showed all the people to Reginald, but they had fled the church.

"'Nothing more 'we' can do?'" Reginald repeated. He shook his head. "No chemotherapy? No operation?"

Dr. Nussbaum looked at him blankly. "The tumor is inoperable." This raised the specter of a pulsing black/red alien growth weaving its way into Reginald's brain.

He didn't know what to do next. He sat there and waited for Dr. Nussbaum to tell him how things would progress from here but Dr. Nussbaum didn't say anything further.

Is he waiting for me to break down, Reginald wondered. Is it appropriate to cry? Dr. Nussbaum had no box of tissues on his desk. The clock on the wall ticked as it jumped ahead one minute. The sound was gunshot loud.

They stared at each other, the doctor and the judge. Reginald knew himself to be superior at the stare-down game. Better than the church game. He had stared down murderers and enemy soldiers and gum-popping waitresses. He was good at it.

"Is there anyone we should call? Your family?" Dr. Nussbaum finally said.

"You or your receptionist?"

"Brandy can make the call, or I can if you like."

"No need. I am alone." His last sentence bounced off the sterile walls. Peggy was 46 years in her grave, bones probably crumbled to dust by now, and any children he might have had died with her. I am alone, he thought. And you, sir, have just sentenced me to die alone. He felt no need to stare down the good doctor anymore. Reginald slumped in the chair for the first time in 70 years. There was no point in playing mental games with Dr. Nussbaum when he had just gotten a death sentence.

"I guess I should go then," Reginald stood up and scraped the chair back. "My fifteen minutes are up anyway."

Dr. Nussbaum stood as well and held out his hand. "I wish you all the best."

At least the doctor had reverted to referring to himself in the first person. "With what? My tumor?"

"No, sir. With the rest of your life." Reginald took the doctor's hand and found a pamphlet between his fingers. The address of a cancer support group.

"And how long will that be?" Reginald looked at the brochure without really seeing it.

"Six months to a year. Make the most of it. If there's something you still want or need to do, go do it."

A roaring started in Reginald's head as he left the inner office. But he was forgetting something. Was this forgetfulness caused by the brain tumor or only the news of it? Or just old age? Maybe he was losing his eidetic memory? He had forgotten to tell Dr. Nussbaum about the auras. He had forgotten to tell Dr. Nussbaum the amputation joke. But it didn't matter. It didn't seem funny anymore anyway. He had forgotten what time it was and he had forgotten to charge his—

Ah, his tablet. That's what he had forgotten. He swept it up from the table in the waiting room, not giving Brandy a second glance. She had probably known his diagnosis all along, and hadn't given him any warning. There was another poor soul reading *Reader's Digest* in the corner, waiting for his turn on the chopping block. "Run," Reginald advised him. "Sprint if you can. There's still time." The patient, an elderly gentleman wearing a floral shirt, stared at him open-mouthed. He had dentures. They were loose. Reginald took his coat and left.

He thought of the picture of the woman on the screen as he tucked the tablet under his arm and started towards his car. It was getting dark already, like it always did in January. And instead of a fresh start for the new year, he had gotten the death penalty. The leftover Christmas lights mocked him. Lucia Zurbriggen of Zermatt, Switzerland. Her face showed no worry wrinkles from war or tragedy or brain tumors. Mountain life must be simple and straightforward, something Reginald could appreciate. He had forgotten to ask Dr. Nussbaum if it would hurt as the tumor progressed. He would have to look it up on the internet.

As he got into his car he felt the weight again of his lucky rock in his pocket. He took it out and examined it. It hat six sides and a pointy tip worn smooth. Over the years in Vietnam and on the bench the crystal had become milky with sorrow, and one of the crystals had broken off. "Some good luck charm you turned out to be." Reginald chucked it out the window into the encroaching winter twilight. How unfair that life had saved its most difficult challenge for his 76th year.

Reginald forced himself to sit upright at his dining table, fighting the urge to slump in defeat. His old bones didn't want to salute any longer. He had put the tablet on the charger, in preparation for all the brain tumor research he was going to do. A cup of tea and the cancer support brochure lay on the table before him. He was now sharing the table with his Diagnosis, the way he was about to share the rest of his life with it, whatever was left of that life.

"If it gets to be too much," a voice in his head suggested, "you can always take the back door exit." Reginald thought of that voice as The Dark Soldier, and the back door exit he was referring to was suicide. Reginald had discussed many things with that faceless voice before.

"I'll keep that in mind," Reginald answered.

He ate and drank all of his meals 'square', hand

with fork or cup lifting directly up from the table and then a right angle into his mouth. He took a sip of tea that way and promptly spit it right back into the cup. It didn't taste like Darjeeling, it tasted like the coffee in Vietnam—as delicious as asphalt. Back then they had applauded every cup of joe, even though it all tasted like airplane exhaust. Vietnam had plenty of tea but coffee had to be imported, and the supply helicopters couldn't always get through. But why was he tasting that now? It must be the brain tumor. He would have to check if appetence hallucinations were a symptom of cancer.

Reginald would usually eat his 'square' meals in the company of the news, either morning, noon or evening. But lately he had become fed up with both Fox News and CNN. Although he was not one to speculate in the stock market, he starting watching MSNBC, which was almost as dry as his toast. He turned on the television. He had to stand up to do it, he didn't own a remote control.

But MSNBC surprised him unpleasantly with a report on some pouting young man from Canada named Justin Bieber. Reginald snapped the television off. His thoughts automatically turned to the past—the coffee in Vietnam, and the last thing Private Miller had said to him. Private Miller had looked a bit like Justin Bieber, only with blue eyes instead of brown.

Reginald had learned to be very careful with his thoughts because of the eidetic memory. It would be dangerous to think about Private Miller or Vietnam too much. He was disciplined, he kept his thoughts close. He had to, so the ugly memories didn't overwhelm his entire life. Dr. Nussbaum had told him that hyperthymesiac patients often suffer from depression, because they were constantly reliving bad memories. Reginald tried never to think about the past, he kept all the important physical souvenirs of his life in a carefully assembled scrapbook. He didn't need to, he remembered the day he graduated from the military academy as if it had only happened hours ago, and every day before that and every day afterwards and if it had rained and what he had eaten for breakfast and all the headlines of every newspaper he had ever read. But the scrapbook was like a file cabinet for him. If he found himself mentally recounting an unpleasant part of his life, he would tell himself that all the details were recorded in the book, and that the book was closed. This helped him redirect his thinking. If he didn't keep his thoughts on a narrow path they would branch off and branch off and branch off again, following slanted tangents that led everywhere. But he was about the open that book.

He retrieved the scrapbook from its faithful spot and took it back to the table. There were some photographs in the album—young Reginald in the Boy Scouts, young Reginald in the army, Reginald with every troop he ever commanded, Reginald draped in his judges' robes. His babyhood had been skipped over completely. There were only two pictures of his mother— a dour woman in the background of a photo of him in his Boy Scout uniform. She wasn't smiling into the lens or beaming proudly at her young son, but scowling at something to the left which wasn't in the picture. That was after his father died. The other picture was tucked into an envelope in the back of the scrapbook, a black and white photograph of his mother and father together, laughing. Taken maybe before he was born. They were barely adults— his mother with her perfectly waved hair looking into the camera and William glancing sideways to her. He tried to avoid looking at the picture but that didn't help because he already knew every detail.

There were some pictures of his fiancée—Peggy— as well, and these were the most dangerous of all. She had died in a car accident while he had been serving in Vietnam, and pictures of her awoke feelings of paralyzing guilt and ghost memories of a life that never was.

The scrapbook had captured his solid career in serving the American people—first as a soldier (Reginald, who loved crosswords and words games appreciated the fact that by changing the letters in 'soldier' around he could make 'solider') and then, after finishing law school and a short career as a prosecutor, as a judge. Reginald had never married and had no children. After he lost his Peggy he never looked for anyone to take her place. He owed it to her memory to remain single, in his mind he was still her finacé. He had been a workaholic before the term was invented, keeping himself busy so he wouldn't have to think too much. He had regarded his troops like his children, raising them very strictly (because most of them came from 'soft' families and where there were awards were given for participation) and he never showed them his emotions. Although he would have died for them.

But he hadn't had the chance to die for Jacob Miller. The one who looked like Justin Bieber. He was pictured in the group portrait of one of the troops Reginald had led in Vietnam. There were 22 young soldiers and Reginald. He had been only a captain then. It looked like a school class photo—the boys were so young. Jacob was in the back, third from the right. His eyes were shaded by his cap and his face looked fuzzy in the aged photo. His freckles weren't visible in the picture. He was what they used to call 'a long drink of water' ... all sinew and bones, floppy like a Raggedey Andy doll. But all Reginald had to do was close his eyes and he saw Jacob Miller lying on the ground, blood bubbling out of his mouth and something horribly wrong with his body. When Reginald first walked up to him, his brain hadn't been able to process what he was seeing. Reginald had had to look twice to see that one of Private Miller's arms was missing and his pelvis had been twisted around. He had led his children into a field full of mines. Reginald hadn't smelled the danger. He had lost three of his boys that day.

The air stank of metal, grease and blood. The freckles stood at attention on Miller's pale face. Reginald had uncharacteristically vomited and then he had knelt beside the dying soldier. He slapped Private Miller's cheek and told him not to be afraid. He would have promised the young man 27 virgins if it would have helped him die well. But before Private Miller died he had something to tell Reginald.

Would he meet Private Miller soon? In heaven? In hell? How would he respond? Private Miller had told him something back then and he had never gotten a chance to ask what he had meant by it.

Reginald had leaned towards him, his ear over his lips. The hot wind, the life leaving him, came out of Private Miller's mouth. Tiny drops of his blood sprayed Reginald's ear. He owed it to Private Miller to listen to his dying statement, but Reginald was afraid that Private Miller would condemn him for murder. He swallowed hard and bent closer.

Private Miller's internal motor was running down. His young body was so twisted, he didn't have a chance. But he had one message: "It is she who will find you." Then he pressed something into Reginald's hand. Then he stopped breathing.

Private Miller had haunted him after that, he hadn't been able to transport Private Miller's dead body out of the jungle, the exploding mines had attracted gunshots and he had to leave the area immediately with the survivors. He had left Private Miller's body behind, but taken a part of Private Miller with him.

Reginald kept watch for a 'she' after that, the one Private Miller had mentioned ... but he didn't find any woman except for a Vietnamese prostitute once on leave. There was no significant other 'she'. Not for more than 50 years.

But why was all this coming back to him now? Was it a sign?

As if in answer, the book that had been next to his scrapbook fell off the shelf. Reginald, startled, got up a little more suddenly than he intended to, banged his thighs on the table and knocked over the chair. The tea-coffee sloshed on the table. He approached the book on the floor and lifted it with love and a superstitious trepidation.

It was the coffee table book of the Swiss mountains. His father William had sent it to his mother as a present from Europe, and it arrived after the telegram announcing his death did. He hadn't died in war, he had fallen to his death from the north face of the Matterhorn. The young widow couldn't afford to have his body flown back, so he was buried in Switzerland. For the mother and son, the book had a supernatural allure, like a gift from the grave. His mother had spent hours looking through that book as she sipped brandy, as if she hoped to find William in one of the photographs.

As Reginald bent down to pick up the book he felt something shift in his pocket. He pulled the crystal out with wonder. "Didn't I throw you away? I was sure I threw you away."

But, like a bad penny, the crystal had turned up again.

Blasted brain tumor, Reginald thought. Had he really thrown his lucky crystal away? Maybe he had only imagined doing it.

This book was old. It was a hardcover with a paper wrapper, a tad ripped, the picture blinding blue and white. As he opened it, something flittered to the floor. Reginald picked it up. It was a photograph of his father, one he had never seen before! His father was standing, hands on his hips, grinning at the camera. The Matterhorn loomed behind him. How had they missed this photo? His mother examined this book thoroughly and never once mentioned this picture.

Unless maybe she had kept it from Reginald on purpose?

Wait a cotton-tailed minute. He laid the picture on the table, mindful of the spilled coffee. He then took his tablet, opened the tab International Science and found the picture of Lucia. He opened the book to page 37. Even without his eidetic memory, he knew all of the pictures by heart.

Both pictures had the same view of the Matterhorn. In the book photograph, there was even a slice of brown in the lower right-hand corner that could have been the aged dark brown wood of the cabin that Lucia stood in front of.

If that wasn't a sign, he didn't know what was.

It is she who will find you.

"If there is something you want or need to do, go do it," Dr. Nussbaum had said.

Instead of researching the symptoms of a brain tumor, Reginald took his tablet and looked up ebookers, searching for flights to Switzerland.

The ringing telephone jolted Cleona awake and she swatted it before she answered it, mistaking it for her alarm, and knocking it to the floor. She groaned as she retrieved it, and it was Marc's voice in her ear: "There's been another explosion." The room came into focus and she struggled to organize her thoughts. Part of her shrieked: "Shut up. Don't tell me anymore." Another part demanded "What? When? Where should I look?" She wedged her mobile between her shoulder and her ear, stood up and started pacing in the small studio apartment in her bra and boxers. Her back was soaked from sleep sweat. The heat had telescoped inside the room and the tacked-up green patterned scarves over the windows had turned the room into a jungle. A cockroach ambled across the floor. A spider scurried on the wall.

"You don't say." Her voice dusky with stolen sleep.

"Well, yes. As a matter of fact I do say." Marc was currently stationed at the Very Large Telescope at the end of Chile. He had once said that that name lacked imagination, he would have called it the Godzilla Telescope or the King Kong Telescope, but Cleona found the original name apt. Static accompanied his every word as his voice wove through the air to her. "It happened at 2:03 Eastern Standard Time last night. We are expecting landfall within in a few hours." He lowered his voice. "It was a big one, Cleona. We can't find the comet anymore with the telescope. The most recent hypothesis is that it's broken apart."

"Any idea where the pieces will fall?"

"Central Europe is the projected trajectory."

"That's not exactly across the street. Nor is it very precise."

"I apologize, but Recce's Comet forgot to consult me before exploding. Of course I would have requested that it land in Guatemala or somewhere closer to you."

Cleona stiffened. "No need to be sarcastic."

"Look, I know how important this is for you and how you've been after this for a long time. All I wanted to do was let you know."

"Sorry, Marc. I know I can be a bitch sometimes."

"At least you admit it," he answered. And that, in a nutshell, was why their relationship had no future. She preferred to live her life according to the Scientific Method. To ask questions, form hypotheses, get proof, draw conclusions. It was a life of constant intellectual curiosity, where Cleona was an active participant. She never held an orange in her hand without wondering where it came from, how it got to her and trying to read its peel bumps like braille. The problem with Marc was that he had just happened to her, and he was chaos personified. He messed up her bed. He made her feel unconcentrated and sticky. He had no place in her formulas. And the conclusions he led her to draw were ones that she preferred not to examine too closely.

"How are you doing?" Marc asked. Cleona closed her eyes. It was a loaded question. She wanted to say "I get scared sometimes. I'm lonely a lot. I wish you were closer. I wish I hadn't been such a jerk. I wish we were together." But instead she said "I'm fine, and yourself?"

"I'm fine too." Static. "Do you think you'll go have a look for the remnants?"

"I don't see how I cannot. I failed to recover anything in Antarctica. This is a second chance for me."

Marc sighed. "Did you ever realize that you are always going to where the scars in the earth are? Wilkes Crater in Antarctica? Chicxulub? Maybe it's because you have so many personal scars of your own."

Cleona pressed her lips together before answering. "Thank you for giving me the information."

"I hope you find what you are looking for." Static. "Well, I won't keep you. I'm sure you are very busy. I just wanted to let you know. Goodbye, Cleona."

"Thank you again, Marc. Goodbye."

She heard one syllable from him as she pushed the disconnect button. Had he wanted to say something else?

She sat back down on her bed staring at the blank face of her mobile. There was no point in calling him back, she told herself. The most important piece of information was already delivered. And just in time! The cockroach was crawling over the letter from Ben Schubert at Borox Corp. It stated that her funding was being reduced after her failure to recover any meteors in Antarctica from Recce's first explosion. Furthermore, if she didn't provide some results, the project would be stopped all together. He didn't even mention her loss of her finger and her toes. He was only interested in a piece of the comet Recce, and Cleo had not delivered.

But this would change everything, she was sure of it.

She put down the mobile and hauled out the star

charts, silently cursing their two-dimensionedness. The paper was damp with Mexican humidity. She would have to calculate, plot and to guess. Her mind raced with mathematical calculations as she put the idea of Marc and that not-understood last word behind her.

After her Antarctican disaster, Cleona had developed tricks—tricks to make her appear closer to 'normal'. She kept her hands busy that people might not notice the tip of the left ring finger was missing. Sometimes, when someone new shook her hand, she kept her glaze locked on theirs and did not blink. She was looking for the question in their eyes—what the hell? Something's wrong here. Her grip was a bit strange due to the missing part of finger. But the strangers soon recovered their poise and were happy to take leave of her strange grip. Sometimes she would hold on for an extra beat just to make things more uncomfortable.

She never wore sandals and only went swimming when she was alone. She always took a private shower after working out—with a door she could close that reached all the way to the floor. She didn't allow herself to explore how much she missed her four lost toes.

Marc had never seen her with her missing digits. She had bid him goodbye before leaving for Antarctica and never re-contacted him after she came back. She was different, and it wasn't only the missing finger and missing toes.

"Chionophobia," her therapist had said.

"What?"

"Intense, irrational fear of snow. That's what you have."

Oh lady, Cleona thought. If you had been through what I have been though you wouldn't think it was so irrational at all.

But there it was. The phobia defied her beloved scientific method, which she applied to all aspects of her life that were difficult, like emotions. And chionophobia didn't fit into Cleo's usual test tube ideology of when something had a name it could be dealt with. Conserved, labelled, corked and stored like her meteor specimens. No. Chionophobia was a sloppy Sasquatch just hiding behind a snow-covered boulder ready to spring. It was so unfair. Along with scoring fairly high on the autism spectrum, she could add an irrational fear of snow to her collection of toys in the attic.

Cleo had solved her problem by moving to Mexico—her dream location near the Chicxulub crater where she could spend her afternoons hunting for impact dust and not thinking of that long, frozen night where she lay on the icy edge of death. Cleona felt best during the day, even in Mexico. She didn't like it when the sun set and darkness crept into the sky.

"Nyctophobia," her therapist had said.

Just great, thought Cleona. Exactly what a comet hunter does not need.

Fear of the night.

Her computer pinged, interrupting her self-diagnosis. The noise was dampened in the sauna-like air of her room. She rolled her chair over to take a look. She was notified every time a news item of interest popped up. She clicked on the article to open it.

A meteorite ... recovered in Switzerland! She studied the woman in the picture. She looked ancient but her face radiated serenity and innocence. She displayed her find proudly. This Swiss lady looked like a solid farm woman, competent but simple. She would be no match for the juggernaut of Cleona's ambition. Cleo would be able to pluck the meteorite out of this woman's hands.

Myths and legends. Stories and fairy tales. Cleona believed none of them. She was the one who complained as a child that there was no way a beanstalk could reach the sky, and, for that matter, a giant certainly couldn't walk on clouds. Clouds were only condensed water drops. And there was no gold at the end of the rainbow. And four-leaf clovers were rather genetic variations in nature than lucky charms.

It was ironic that such a woman made her living out of chasing fallen stars.

Chapter 3

A few days after the meteorite struck earth, it began snowing. Fat flakes drifted down in the night as Lucia lay restless in her bed and Sparky kept guard by the window. She watched the ceiling without seeing it, musing that it hadn't taken long for journalists to discover where the meteorite had landed and who had almost been clocked by it. The light and the noise must have caused quite a stir in town. But she figured that the media storm was over and the snow would protect her. The snow absorbed sound and the world around her had fallen silent.

At the crash site the intense heat from the meteor had somehow burned the snow in the impact area into a strange kind of hot crystal ice, but that was being covered up by fresh powder, along with all the journalists' tracks—everything wiped clean for a fresh start. By the time the sun came up, burning off the fluffy snow clouds, 20 cm of new powder covered the landscape, taking the edge of the cliffs and spiky rocks. A skiers dream, Lucia thought as she peered out the window. She hadn't donned skis herself for ten years, her bones were too fragile.

The window glass had become a bit warped over time, bending the landscape into gentle hills and swirls. The sunlight threw everything into stark relief—shadows were deep against the brilliance of the snow and it hurt her eyes to look at the scenery for too long. Snowblindness was a real risk in the mountains. Several of her childhood friends had suffered from various degrees of the affliction, sometimes running head first into boulders during games of hide-and-seek.

Lucia took a step back so her breath wouldn't fog the window up. Her memory must be failing. She couldn't remember how long she had lived in this house. She couldn't remember what her mother looked like. She couldn't remember the name of her last dog. And she couldn't remember—something else. She patted Sparky's flank. "I am getting old."

An alpine clough, one of the few birds Lucia knew, called a warning. Suddenly the earth lurched under Lucia's feet and from high on a peak on a mountain across from her house a tiny snowball started its way to the valley. As it rolled it gathered mass, which merged together to form a sliding sheet of snow, snow dust tossed into the air, a rolling cloud weighing tons. White death. Lucia watched the avalanche slide down the mountain towards the valley like a Mountain God's judgement on the people below.

Avalanches weren't an unusual occurance, and most of them were harmless. But she had a strange feeling as she watched the snow race down the slope. Even though the journalists who had snapped pictures and asked banal questions were gone, she had the feeling something else was coming. Something even bigger than an avalanche. Even bigger than a meteorite. Something. And she didn't know whether to be happy or afraid.

Amanda Bennett (née Carthage) and her teenage son, Zachary, were riding in a train snaking its way up the mountain towards Zermatt. She was studying a map of the area, awkwardly spread across the small table and her lap. As a child, she had kept a Rand-McNally Atlas by her bed and before she fell asleep she studied the highways and capital cities of all the states. Every place in America was connected. There was a way TO everywhere, and a way FROM. Even if you turned in the wrong direction you could hang a right at the next block and box yourself back in the correct direction. Or you could get off at the next exit and re-enter the highway going the other way.

Switzerland didn't work like that at all. There were roads here that just ended. Ended in what? Amanda was curious. She traced a Swiss road with her fingertip, nail ragged from being chewed. Studying the map was an excellent distraction from looking at the sullen teenager slumped across from her. She didn't even mind that the huge foldout map must make her look old-fashioned to all the other passengers on the train. Most people had Google Maps on their smart phones. But she used the extra-large paper to block her view of son's face.

She wasn't sure how long she had been studying the map but she was starting to run out of dead end roads. She tried to fold it back up the way it was supposed to be folded, failed, and crumpled it up instead, shoving it back in her purse.

There was a woman across from her with black hair cut in a geometrically severe bob. Such sharp angles weren't usually found in hairstyles. She might have been of Asian descent, except she had dark blue eyes, magnified by glasses. Her eyes frowned at the edges of her lids, giving her an effect of permanent sadness. She had a huge steel case beside her that didn't fit under the seat and partially blocked the aisle. Next to her on the window seat was a young mother across from her daughter. The little girl was babbling in German to a Barbie she was holding, brushing Barbie's long blonde locks with a pink plastic hairbrush. Next to the young girl was a stiff-looking older man, who wasn't amused by the Barbie and kept giving the case annoyed glances. It seemed to be taking up some of his leg room. Amanda looked out the window before she could catch anyone's eye and watched the landscape.

The Swiss Alps had a deep 'can't get there from here' feel. Once they were on the train from Visp going up to Zermatt there was no way to turn around, like she had observed on the map. The train track ran parallel to a feisty stream splashing with minty green water. They rumbled past a few mountain ghost towns, small empty buildings whose tiny windows looked like eyes, watching the tourists parade up and down the mountain. Amanda couldn't even guess what the purpose of these buildings was. Basically the train track was just a glorified ramp going up and up and up, final destination Zermatt. After that there was nothing, at least not on Amanda's map.

She had run out of distractions. She sighed and turned to her son. He needed a shampoo and a haircut. His greasy brown bangs hid one of his eyes and most of the pimples on his forehead. He was texting with a two-thumbed technique. Her heart turned over. She had loved him so much, and she barely knew him anymore.

He was so absorbed in his phone that she had the rare opportunity to study him. The light from the screen bathed his features in a bluish glow. Strange how his face had stretched and grown to the edge of being a young man, whiskers bristling at his chin, blackheads nested next to his nose. He was 16 now. At 15 he had still been hers. To some extent. But 16 was new territory. And after his arrest and the lawyers and the court, she no longer had any idea who he had become.

She hoped to change that. She had gotten him to come along on this trip, through bribery, tears, pleading and threats. It had been a tough grind, getting him to agree. She might as well to try to enjoy the trip herself. It was expensive enough, actually more than she could afford.

Amanda fished around in her purse for her paperback. She came up with her wallet instead. There was a wrinkled twenty-dollar bill, 400 in Swiss francs and an almost maxed-out Master Card, along with Zach's primary school picture. Time had stopped in her wallet. She traced his young face as she had traced the roads. He was smiling at her from the past. Where had her little boy gone?

Zach groaned and put his phone on the seat beside him. "Mom, you got a cable?"

Amanda froze. A chance! The grump-statue has spoken! She tucked the picture back into her wallet. She wasn't going to miss this opportunity. "No, I'm sorry, honey. I don't."

"Shit. My battery's low." He put his forehead on the window and then jerked it away. "Hey, that's cold!"

"Welcome to the real world." Amanda wanted to eat the words as soon as they were out. Especially her tone. It sounded bitchy. Fortunately Zach seemed not to care. His day was ruined by the lack of cable. "So, what's going on at home?" she asked.

Zachary shrugged his shoulders and stared out the window.

"When we get to Zermatt, we'll have to rent you some skis."

No reaction.

"Or would you rather stick to your snowboard?"

Zach shrugged again.

"Skis might be safer. We should also organize some lessons for you. I hear they have good ski schools up there."

Zach rolled his eyes. "Where did you pack the cable?"

"In the suitcase."

Zach stood up and heaved the suitcase down from the overhead bin. It was awkward and he didn't have any room to open it and search through it. Amanda noted the passengers on the other side of the aisle observing him. The serious-looking woman seemed particularly intrigued by his struggle. Zachary gave up, shoved the suitcase back onto the overhead rack and plopped back down, scowling.

"You packed really well Mom. Why didn't you put the cable on top or in the side pocket? That would have made sense."

"I'm sorry." Amanda felt her prospect of communicating with him ebbing away. "Maybe next time you can help me with the packing. You seem to think about things I don't, I'm sure I could learn a lot from you."

"There won't be a next time." He turned to stare out the window.

The train braked suddenly and Amanda's coffee spilled onto Zach's leg.

"Oh, I'm sorry, honey. Here, let me help you." She fished out the wadded-up map out of her purse and started blotting his jeans with it.

He brusquely brushed her hand away. "Mom, leave me alone!"

Amanda froze, not knowing how to react. She felt the eyes of the old man and the woman across the aisle on her. Did they feel pity? Disgust? Amanda shoved the map back into her purse and blinked back hot tears. Zach was busy staring at his dead smart phone, not even looking at her. His iPod was apparently still working though. He put in his ear buds. The music was so loud that she could make out the lyrics of the song he was listening to. Something about bitches and throwing around hundreds. She guessed the other passengers could hear it as well, but it was no use telling him to turn it down. He wouldn't comply and it would only make her look more like the ineffective parent that she was.

Instead she looked outside to see if she could make

out why they had stopped so suddenly. There was a river of snow that had tumbled down the mountain, fresh, crossing the tracks somewhere ahead of them.

The hardy construction workers of Valais, equipped with the most modern aerodynamic shovels, but only shovels nonetheless, were already working on it. Avalanches must not be that uncommon for the area. They had gone to work as soon as the sun lit the Matterhorn like a big fat birthday candle, and continued working as the golden orange light creeped down the slope. Import tourists, export tourists. It was all in a day's work.

*

Zachary watched the workers too, forehead not quite resting against the window of the train, with a mixture of admiration and disgust. They looked so carefree, laughing and joking as they shoveled the white stuff away, but what stupid work. When he was twelve, Zach had shoveled his neighbor's driveway to make extra pocket money. Had he been happy to do it? He couldn't remember. These days when he looked in the mirror (and he tried hard not to ever have to, unless something was stuck in his teeth or a pimple needed popping), his eyes displayed only the eternal boredom which had become his standard look. He put on his bored face as soon as he stood up every morning. It was his defense, a good one, that neither his mother, nor his father nor the teachers nor the counselor nor the psychiatrist nor the police had been able to penetrate.

He watched shovels full of snow arc in the morning sun. He had to shift his position because he dreaded having to look at his mother, to see that sad but hopeful expression she always wore. He hated her face. He sometimes wanted to hit her, just so that look would go away. Of course he would never do anything like that, but she sensed that he wanted to and he knew that she knew, so it was always between them—that unthrown punch that hung in the air. He opened a Snickers bar and the sweet taste flooded his mouth, trying to chew the feeling away.

His mother tapped him on his coffee-damp knee. He instinctively jerked it away and she looked wounded enough as if he had gone ahead and punched her. He yanked his earphone out of his ear.

"What?"

"Here," she said. She thrust a chocolate bar at him. "We are in Switzerland, after all. I thought you might like to eat some real Swiss chocolate."

Zach felt temper rising but tried to squash it. "I just opened this one, Mom. I don't want to eat that one too. I might get fat ... ." He let that roll off, implying but not quite saying that his mother had a weight problem. She actually didn't, not in Zach's eyes, she was over 40 and her body had sunken into more of a blubbery pear shape in recent years.

His mom was hurt anyway. He couldn't say anything right to her, there was no point in trying.

*

The workmen, having freed the track from snow, stepped aside to wave at the passengers. Amanda's eyes were wet with tears, these strangers more friendly than her own son. She shook her head. She hated this part of her that was so sensitive. She was weak. Her ex-husband Steve had also said so. This trip had been a horrible idea. What had she been thinking? It had only just started and it was going to be a nightmare.

Then they chugged around the bend and she gasped, forgetting how upset and wounded she was. At first she thought it wasn't real. Something was wrong with the horizon. She blinked. It was still there. The Matterhorn. She had only seen it in books. Until now. The village of Zermatt nestled at the Matterhorn's feet radiating charm and quaintness. The mountain that looked unreal, like something that someone had placed there, like something built, and turned the whole town into some kind a movie set.

This is a place of power, Amanda thought. A place of dreams. She dared to hope again.

Cleona sat ramrod straight in the uncomfortable train seat. She had tried to prepare herself for the journey. She had, at the advice of her therapist, forced herself to look at pictures of winter landscapes in the mountains and practiced calm breathing and muscle relaxation—a sort of self-hypnosis. Those endless stretches of glittering crystal fields, diamonds that disappeared when you tried to hold them in your hand, and when the wind blew the air was full of glitter dust. She knew how deadly snow could be. The avalanche that brought the train to a halt was a reminder. Or a warning.

Why Zermatt of all places? Why couldn't the meteorite have landed in the Sahara, where at least it was warm? And why winter? When all the ugly snow covered the wonderful rocks? Searching for lazulite in summer, a mineral specific to Zermatt, would have been easier, and more fun, but the meteor was Cleona's passion.

As the train chugged onward to Zermatt, she distracted herself by the drama happening in the seats across from her, a fluttery mother travelling with her dour teenage son. What a horror. Cleo was not a parent by her own choice. She could dissect a pebble of a meteorite layer by layer over a time period of three months or more, analyzing it down to the individual crystals to the proteins to amino acids to atoms to electrons to proteins and down to types of quarks—up, strange, charmed. But she had zero patience with people, and negative patience for children.

There was a little pig-tailed girl sitting across from Cleona, staring at her and sucking her lollipop. She held a Barbie in one sticky hand. Cleo shifted uncomfortably in her seat. She knew all about mineral composition. She knew nothing about how to handle little girls.

"That's a cool bag," the girl said in her primary school English. She nudged Cleona's case with her pink shoe. "What you got in it?"

Cleona winced when the shabby unicorn sneaker

touched her pristine case but dutifully picked it up and put it on her lap. She opened it. Full of sample jars, tubes of acid, tweezers, picks, small hammers. The girl's eyes grew to the size of pancakes. "What's all that for?"

"Torture," answered Cleo.

As she looked into the little girl's frightened eyes, she thought of herself as a young girl. Cleona hadn't been interested in unicorns and Barbies. She had been interested in chemistry from the get-go.

She remembered how, at seven, she had found her adoptive mother Linda staring at herself in the bathroom mirror. Linda was greying at the temples and above her forehead and she smelled like an open bottle of white wine left out in the sun. Patting her stomach and moaning softly, she opened the mirrored cabinet and took out Rolaids. When she closed it again she was surprised by Cleona standing in the doorway, clutching a pink piece of chalk.

"Jesus kid you frightened me."

Cleona cocked her head to one side. She understood almost everything Linda said now but her language still sounded flat and nasal to Cleona. Cleona had dressed herself that morning in a Big Bird T-shirt with Levis and screaming yellow sneakers, looking typically American. But she still had the power to startle Linda, as if Linda, even after one year, wasn't used to having a child around. Cleo (Linda and Bud had started calling her that, and soon she was thinking of herself with that name, her American name) had a tendency to just appear in random places, as if from some other dimension, her head tilted as if she were an alien who didn't quite understand where she was.

"Is that candy?" Cleo pointed at the Rolaids.

"No, hun. That's medicine for my-m-ommy's tummy." Linda always stuttered a bit over the 'mommy' part. She wasn't fooling Cleona. She wasn't even fooling herself.

"Oh I have that too!" Cleona held up her chalk. "I was drawing outside with it."

Linda smiled. "What were you drawing, hun? A house? A cat?"

"A DNA molecule."

Linda nodded as if that were the most normal thing in the world.

"That's nice, honey. But that's a piece of chalk. This is medicine for sick tummies. It's not the same."

"Sure it is. They are both cal-ci-um car-bon-ate."

Linda sighed and popped a Rolaid into her mouth. She chewed thoughtfully as she peered at the Rolaids wrapper.

"You're right, honey. Calcium carbonate. And this tastes just like your chalk too." Linda stuck out her pink tongue, perhaps hoping to elicit a giggle from Cleona but she just stared at her adoptive mother solemnly. "By the way, Cleo, have you seen my jewelry box? It's missing from my dresser."

Cleo looked at the floor and jiggled one of her legs. "Um, yeah, it's on my desk."

"Honey, if you want to borrow my jewelry, you can ask. I have no problem if you want to wear my necklaces around the house."

"I don't want to wear it, I want to examine it."

"What?"

"One of the diamonds in your ring is black. Not really black in color, more like grey, but in my ge-o-lo-gee book it's called black. The book says that these are car-bon-a-dos, and they could have pieces of meteors in them!"

"And how do you propose to find that out?" Linda asked.

"Acid test."

"Miss Cleona Skye!" Linda stamped her foot, sour stomach forgotten. "You give me back my ring right now!"

Cleona smiled at the memory and tried to catch the gaze of the little girl with the Barbie again, form a kinship. The little girl refused to look at Cleona, focusing on her mother instead, imploring her with desperate eyes.

"Excuse us," the mother said huffily in accented English. She took Barbie Girl by the hand and they left the train car. The little girl shot Cleona one last look of fright before being dragged off by her mother.

"Really put a scare into that little lass, didn't you?" asked the old man sitting across from her.

Cleona sighed. She had failed again with human contact. Why couldn't people just be formulas where you plug in the right numbers and come out with the result? Oh well, with Miss Unicorn gone, at least she had more room for her case.

Chapter 4

The train pulled into Zermatt, spilling passengers with their baggage out onto the platform— awkward jumbles of suitcases, skis and boots. Cleona only had two small bags with her, one with her clothes and the silver one with her equipment. She always travelled light—her short cropped hair needed no styling products, she didn't wear makeup, she didn't own many clothes. Cleo was streamlined for science, always ready for the next adventure. She dodged her way out of the train station into the sun, away from the creepy old man, nervous mother and grumpy son. She stopped short as soon as she caught sight of the snow, but it wasn't so bad in town, more a grey-brown mush. The mountains would be the real challenge.

The station had the feel of a well-oiled conveyer belt—the turnover of passengers embarking and disembarking. The empty-wallet tourists replaced by the full-wallet ones, only to do the same dance next week. It was a funny kind of waltz, the pale faces sidestepping off the train as the suntanned ones boarded. Skis clicked together as they passed. Suitcases bumped.

Zach watched his Mom struggle out of the train with their baggage. He knew she didn't dare to ask him for help because he would turn her down and, in addition, use it as a reason to bitch about the trip.

She would be humiliated in public, again. Zach didn't care anymore about what people thought of him, but he knew that his mother was conscious of her public image and he used that knowledge to his advantage whenever it served him.

Amanda built a tower of suitcases on the platform and propped Zach's snowboard against it, wiping the sweat from her forehead. All that lifting in her winter clothes among so many people had turned her into a furnace. Her jacket and thermal underwear had been real finds at the thrift shop, but had probably been last used in Siberia. She scanned the area. She couldn't manage to get everything out of the train station to get a taxi by herself. Then she watched as another family trundled past them, all their luggage balanced precariously on a trolley.

"Zachary, could you be a dear and get us a trolley?" Her voice had an edge, daring him to turn her down. There it was, the request for help. The challenge.

Zach stared at her. "Why should I?"

"Because," and she sighed her eternal martyr's sigh, "you don't have to be a genius to see I cannot manage this all by myself."

"Make several trips," Zach suggested. "That's exactly what you told me when you made me clear the table and I was too little to fight back."

Amanda's face got red, her emotions bulging behind their sturdy locked gates. "Look, this vacation is for you, too. It's costing me a fortune. The least you could do is get me a trolley." Pushing the guilt button now.

"Get it yourself." Zach fiddled with his earphones. "I'll wait here with the luggage."

"If you get it, I'll load it and push it. Deal? All I want is for you to get it. Is that so difficult?"

"Yes."

"Well, I'm not moving without a trolley, so I guess we'll be here all day."

"Guess so."

Two could play the power game, but it always was a stalemate. Things had changed since Zach had grown taller than Amanda. Since he had beat her in arm wrestling. Since his arrest.

Zachary looked at her, his expression neutral. She needed a haircut. Her jolly snow hat with an outrageous rainbow pom-pom affixed to the top pushed her hair down over her eyes and counterpointed her pale face and twitching mouth. He waited a good minute and a half to let her simmer, and then an extra half-minute for good measure, before he slunk off. Let her wonder if he was going to get a trolley or just disappear. Actually he didn't care enough to continue sparring with her. He just wanted to get through one thing so he could get to another thing so he could get to another thing. His life had turned into a chain of events just to get through. All the feelings were gone, Zachary was emotionally flatline. As he approached the trolleys he saw that there was a line to get one. I'm definitely not waiting fifteen minutes for a fucking trolley, he thought. He waited on the side and as soon as a harried father deposited one Zach moved to grab it.

He felt a hand on his arm. He spun around, already in fight or flight mode, and was confronted by the old man who had been sitting across from them in the train. He grabbed Zachary's arm with a surprisingly strong grip for an old geezer. He spoke to Zach animatedly and was shaking his finger. Zach shook the man's hand from his arm and pulled out one of his earphones. "I didn't hear you."

"The queue starts back there," the man pointed to the back of the line.

"I don't know what a fucking queue is. I'm from America, there we have lines. I'm a visitor here, and I'm definitely not waiting in any line!"

It was a stare down. The man's watery blue eyes probed the boy's brown ones. "I'm an American too. And Americans act as ambassadors for their own country."

Zach brushed roughly past him, wrestled the trolley free and stomped off.

"You give your country a bad name, young sir!" The old man called after him. Zach stuck his earphones back in.

Zachary approached his mother, who had worry etched between her eyes in deep lines. "What was that about?"

"Look, you wanted the damn trolley, here it is!" He shoved it at her, the dramatic effect hampered by the automatic brake.

"Zachary! We are guests in this country. We have to respect their ways. And their rules."

"What are you, buddies with that old guy over

there? Who gives a fuck what you think? So don't ask me for any more favors!" Zach turned up his music, and watched as his mother, blinking back hot tears and biting back anguished sobs, loaded the trolley.

*

Amanda had always loved maps but hated puzzles, and trying to fit all the baggage on the trolley was a task she had no interest in. The theme from Tetris played in her head as she put two suitcases next to each other and jamming a duffle bag on top. Anything to distract her from her son's flat stare and stave off the nibbling nervous breakdown. Zach's snowboard was awkward and slippery, seemed to weigh about 700 pounds, and did not fit in the slots meant for skis.

Could you help me with this, she almost asked, but bit that back as well. She had already been punished for daring to ask him for a favor. She tried to jam the snowboard into the slot.

It refused to fit.

She sighed hotly and wedged the snowboard between Zach's suitcase and her own, wondering how she would ever survive this trip. The heat pressed out from inside her and was blocked by her clothes, reflected back and doubled. I am a walking greenhouse effect, she thought and almost laughed. Menopause already? But Zachary's constant contempt was wearing down her heart and her humor, it was getting more and more difficult to find things funny and to laugh.

Finally she got everything on the trolley, the handle in one hand, the other hand clamped between the snowboard and the suitcase. The cart kept automatically breaking as she inched out of the train station. She hitched her way to the street, into the sunlight, where hundreds of other visitors to Zermatt were trying to catch electric taxis. She looked back anxiously to see if Zachary was following her. He was hanging back far enough that no one could guess they were together, his gaze locked on his iPod.

Amanda took a deep breath and the air crackled in her lungs. She maneuvered her cart next to a smart, serious-looking woman with short hair. Amanda recognized her as the woman sitting across from them on the train. Her silver suitcase was blinding in the sunlight. The woman was calmly raising her arm to call for a taxi. Amanda raised her arm too, but had to put it back down to catch the snowboard from falling. She noted the luggage tags on the woman's suitcase. She smiled. "Are you American? Going to Hotel Bergkrystall?"

"Yes." The woman looked puzzled. "How did you know?"

"The tags on your luggage. That's our hotel too." Amanda held out her hand. "I'm Amanda Bennett. My son is Zachary." She nodded at Zach, who didn't even look up.

"I'm Cleona Syke." She shook Amanda's hand with short, capable pumps.

Amanda grimaced at the strange grip and noticed that Cleona Skye was missing a finger. She wiped her hand on her jeans unconsciously after letting go just in time to grab the snowboard again, which kept slipping. "Where are your skis?"

"I don't ski. I'm a geologist. I'm here to recover a meteorite."

A taxi skidded to a halt right in front of Cleona, although she had no longer been raising her hand. She must look like an attractive fare, with hardly any luggage, Amanda thought.

"Well, see you at the hotel." She moved to open the door and then stopped. "Unless you would like to share a cab?"

Amanda was so grateful that her smile jittered at the edges and tears gathered in the corners of her eyes. "That's very kind."

Cleo started towards the massive pile of luggage to help load it when an older man pushed past her and, slick as oil, got in the cab.

"Excuse me, sir," Cleo said. "This taxi is ours." She looked at him and noticed that it was the older man who had been sitting across from her on the train. "If you think I can scare little girls just wait until you see what I can do to senior citizens."

"I believe that you are outside the taxi, miss. And now I am sitting in it. It's my fare," Reginald said. The taxi driver looked at Cleona and shrugged.

Cleo lifted her chin and looked indignant. "That's not very polite."

"Neither is he. Ask him." Reginald pointed to Zachary, who had stopped playing with his iPod long enough to witness the drama. Reginald tipped an imaginary hat at the trio and directed the driver in German. The taxi trundled off.

"What is it I should ask you?" Cleona said to Zachary.

"How much I love Switzerland," Zach said. "What an asshat."

Cleo waved down another taxi. She had an authoritative way of standing there holding her arm only at half-mast, but she called the taxi to her like a mistress calls her obedient dog. The taxi driver and Cleona helped Amanda load the baggage. Cleo did most of the work, fitting all the suitcases into a practically perfect cube. Even the taxi driver, an expert baggage loader, seemed impressed.

"Are you good at Tetris?" Amanda asked.

"I'm good at geometry," Cleo corrected.

Zachary got in without helping. It wasn't like any taxi he had been in before, with two benches facing each other.

Amanda and Cleona also piled in the taxi, the women sharing one bench across from Zach. Zach caught Cleo studying him and frowning.

She did not seem embarrassed at all to be caught. She met his eyes without flinching. "Why didn't you help with the suitcases?"

"Because I don't give a fuck."

Amanda opened her mouth, to make an excuse for his behavior, but there was no explanation so she just closed her mouth again. She used to joke about his swearing, admonishing him to 'sit on' his language, rather than just to watch it. But she hadn't dared to scold him for a long time. "Can you speak German?" she asked Cleo instead.

"Yes. German is the language of scientists, French of politicians."

"Only assholes speak German," Zachary commented. Cleo noticed the cab driver stiffen. "Fucking Nazis."

"The Swiss were actually neutral in World War Two, they certainly weren't Nazis." Cleo continued to examine Zach as if he were some sort of alien insect. "Your luggage is bulky and fairly massive." She looked directly at him.

"So what?"

"You are taller than your mother, and you are male in gender, so you are probably stronger too."

"And?"

"I'm trying to figure out why you aren't helping more with your suitcases. "

"That's no mystery. I told you. I don't want to be here, and I simply don't give a fuck."

Amanda gasped but Cleona didn't flinch. "You are thoroughly the living stereotype of the angry teenager. You are a caricature of yourself. I've never met someone like you."

"Leave me the fuck alone."

"He's had a rough go of it lately," Amanda broke in. "He's been in trouble with the law—"

"Shut up, Mom! What are you going to do? Tell everybody?"

Cleo leaned forward, hands dangling between her knees. "I study rocks, not people. I don't have any children. I don't have contact with teenagers. I did not

54

mean to offend you. It's just obvious that you worked for the money to pay for exactly none of this vacation and yet you let your own mother play your porter." She turned to Amanda. "Is he blackmailing you?"

Amanda blinked back hot tears. She didn't know whether or not to be relieved or mortified that this total stranger was addressing the elephant in the room. "Why do you ask?"

"I can't figure out why you would let yourself be treated like this. Maybe he has something on you."

Oh he has, Amanda thought. If only you knew. He's holding my heart hostage.

Mercifully they pulled up in front of the hotel.

It was a strong, solid but rather unremarkable two-story building, built like a treasure chest to protect the jewels inside from the bitter winter. As the taxi pulled up to the lobby door, Amanda's arm froze on the way to the door handle. "Uh-oh."

There was already a taxi in front of theirs and Reginald was disembarking and giving the driver orders on how to unpack the baggage. He gave them a jolly wave as the driver loaded things onto the porter's cart.

"He stole the porter, too," Amanda remarked.

"Don't worry about that. By the time we've unloaded all your baggage, the porter be back and ready for us," Cleona said. "Why don't you go ahead on in? You can check in while the driver unpacks your things and by the time you're done the porter will be back." Cleona commiserated with this woman. She could definitely use a break.

"Thank you Ms. Skye. Ms.? Mrs.? Miss?"

"Actually Its Dr. Skye, but people I know call me Cleo for some reason I cannot fathom." She started unpacking the baggage, top items first. The taxi driver had given up and lit a cigarette and watched her work.

Amanda's eyes dampened again at the unexpected kindness. She was wet and soppy at the edges. "Thank you, Cleo."

"Don't thank me." Cleo waved her off. "It's definitely more efficient this way."

It was impossible to judge the size of the hotel from the front. The façade facing the street only had five windows and a double door entrance. The two story building seemed to stretch far back into the side of the mountain, like a lodge. It was built from solid red bricks, the balconies were white with gold railings. Amanda caught a glimpse of an outdoor Jacuzzi on the left side, steam rising into the sky.

Zachary trailed his mother into the snug hotel reception area. Amazing chunks of crystal were displayed in mirrored cabinets. The upholstery on the two chairs in the lobby was red velvet look with worn gold buttons set in mahogany wood. The bookshelf held rows of unlabeled books with deep blue covers and gold inlays. Zach didn't see the dog sprawled across the carpet, tripped over it, and fell face first on the floor.

The lady proprietor rushed forward and Amanda could see the concern for her beloved pet in her body language but she forced herself to go to Zachary first. "Are you all right, young man?"

"Yes," Zach said briskly. He sat up.

She turned to Amanda. "Welcome to the Hotel Bergkrystall, Mrs. Bennett! My name is Claudia Andermatt and I am most honored to have you here. I must say, you have made quite an entrance."

"It's Ms. Bennett," Zach's mother said, buzzing the 's' on Ms. like a bee. "But please call me Amanda."

Zachary was in no hurry to stand up. He reached out and stroked the dog, who looked to be about 100 years old and was still asleep, seemingly unaware that Zach had just taken a face plant over him.

"Her name is Askia. She's 16 years old. So am I. We grew up together."

Zach looked up. A girl towered over him, blue eyes glimmering with good humor.

"Can I help you up?" she asked in English peppered with something sweet and German-y.

"No, thanks, I'm all right." Zachary bounded up and discovered that he was a full two heads taller than this girl. She had seemed larger from his position on the floor. He tried to brush the dog hair off him.

"I'm Emma Andermatt." She extended a small yet capable hand. Her thick, honey-colored hair was pulled up in a sloppy ponytail and wayward strands had escaped to frame her face.

"Zachary Bennett." Felt weird to shake her hand. Did kids do that in Switzerland?

"You like snowboarding?" She pointed to his snowboard leaning against the door.

"Yes." It didn't seem prudent to admit he was only a beginner.

"Did you sign up for a course already? My mom can help you with that."

"That would be gr—"

"Or I could show you the area. I know all the best trails." She smiled.

"N-no thanks," Zach stammered and looked away. He pulled the bored mask down over his features again. Emma's face just fell, there was no other word for it. Her brilliant smile wavered and her eyebrows arched with questions.

But it was better this way, he thought as he pushed past her and reinserted his earphone. He flopped down in one of the chairs and stared at his iPod while his mother discussed something he couldn't hear with Mrs. Andermatt. The girl didn't know what he had done. If she did she would cower behind the reception desk, shaking. She didn't know that he was a monster.

Chapter 5

A manda was struggling to keep her expression neutral, as if the beauty around her was as ordinary as orange juice in the morning. She didn't know how anyone could manage to cram so much crystal into the dining area without being melodramatic, but somehow the Andermatts had done it. It was a magical fairy princess room, every little girl's dream. Only the unicorn was missing. Candles flicked on all the tables and their light was reflected and refracted from every corner. It was as if all the stars had fallen to earth and had been remounted in this room. Her stomach rumbled at the fine smells wafting from the kitchen, a sensory compliment to all the colored light. It was all a huge leap up from the oily chain restaurants she was used to.

She was met at the doorway by Fraulein Emma Andermatt. Emma's ponytail was now tidied into a French roll and she held her clipboard competently. "Good evening, Ms. Bennett. May I bring you to your table?" Her smile faded as she glanced behind Amanda and caught sight of Zach, but she maintained a grip on her professionalism—an impressive feat for a 16-year-old girl. Zach had managed to charge his smart phone and was no longer bothering to look up for anyone or anything.

Amanda nodded, she didn't trust herself to speak,

and followed Emma through the labyrinth of tables to where Cleona was sitting.

"Your seat, ma'am." Emma pulled out the chair for Amanda.

"Oh, I'm sorry, there's some mistake." Amanda looked at Cleo. "We're not together."

Emma looked puzzled. "But you arrived together."

"We were only sharing a taxi."

"Oh I do apologize! I will set up another table for you immediately!"

"There's no need for that." Cleo put down her napkin, which had strange creases from being folded and refolded. "I don't mind the company."

"Are you sure?" Amanda asked.

"Positive." Amanda turned to Emma. "We'll sit here, then, thanks." Emma beamed and bounced off to get the menus.

"Wouldn't want to get the young lady in trouble, would we now, Zachary?" Cleo asked him.

Zach collapsed into a chair. He didn't bother to answer and his gaze never left his iPhone.

"Sorry about this," Amanda said. "Thanks for letting us sit with you."

Cleo took a sip of water before responding. "I hope I am good company. I am used to eating alone."

Amanda glanced at Zach and couldn't bite back the comment. "I am, too."

"I believe she is too." Cleo nodded at an older lady seated alone in the corner. She wore a black-sequined dress and a chucky gemstone necklace. Every finger sported a sparkling ring. Her tent dress gave no clue as to her figure, but she looked solid. Her hair was sprayed into perfect swirls, her makeup and nails were immaculate. However, she seemed to be having an animated conversation with her silverware.

"I wonder why she is by herself," Amanda mused.

"That's Vera Buxomburger," Emma had reappeared, passing out the menus, filling their water glasses and keeping her voice low. "Every year her husband drops her off so he can have a week's holiday from her. I think he goes to the Caribbean with his girlfriend. But we look after her while she's here."

"Do you think you should be speaking so freely about your guests?" Cleo asked.

Emma blushed and straightened. Zachary turned on Cleo, snarling. "Leave her the fuck alone."

"Zachary!" Amanda scolded.

"Aha," Cleo mused. "Apparently the Young and Angry does actually care about something."

"C-can I bring you something else to drink?" Emma changed the subject.

"I'll have a glass of white wine, please," Amanda said. "A big one."

"Beer," Zach said.

"Zachary! You're only sixteen!"

"Sixteen, right. The legal drinking age in Switzerland."

"He'll have a Coke," Amanda told Emma.

"Mineral water," Cleo said, trying to keep the amusement from creeping into her voice.

"I'll be right back with your drinks." Emma walked away, her sashay had lost most of its swing.

"You didn't have to take her down like that." Zach pointed his knife at Cleo.

"Zachary! Put that knife down. Right now!"

"I found it inappropriate," Cleo said coolly. "How would you like it if she went over to that family over there and started talking about you?"

"I wouldn't give a fuck."

"Well, now, Cleona," Amanda desperately broke in. "Why don't you tell us why you're here? I want to hear more about that meteorite."

Zach had swung his knife around. "Look, there's that asshole." The women looked up and saw the gaunt old man march into the dining room and take a seat. He smiled at them and tipped his imaginary hat.

"I'm going to shove his fucking imaginary hat up his skinny ass," Zach grumbled.

Cleo grinned a little. "I would be interested in observing that, young sir." She turned to Amanda. "I'm here to collect my piece of heaven. That's why I came."

"You're right," Amanda looked around the dining room. "It is very beautiful. I've never been in such a fancy hotel."

"No, not because of the hotel. I'm looking for a piece of heaven that fell to earth—a meteorite."

Cleo took a picture clipped from a magazine out of her briefcase. She handed it to Amanda. It was of a smiling old woman holding a rock in her outstretched hand. A friendly-looking dog was sitting beside her. "This woman discovered the meteor. I'm going to find her. I think I can triangulate her location from the mountains depicted in the background."

Amanda frowned and flipped the picture over. "Doesn't it say somewhere in the article who she is?"

"I cut that part out, but I already memorized it. Lucia Zurbriggen. It doesn't list her address, but I found out which mountains are behind her, and they are here above Zermatt. I brought good hiking boots and tomorrow I will go visit Madame Zurbriggen."

Amanda handed the picture back to Cleo. "What makes the meteorite special?"

"Three days ago the comet Recce approached the sun, and it's outgassing caused it to explode. The meteorite is probably a piece from this comet."

"Outgassing," Zach tittered. Amanda rolled her eyes and nodded at Cleona to continue.

"Recce is an ancient comet with a red, silver and gold tail indicating a high silicate content. Due to the angle of its eccentricity, I believe that Recce comes from outside our solar system. Just imagine, it's still impossible for man to travel outside the solar system. How fortunate that a piece has come to us. I have been following the progress of this comet with great interest. It has always behaved strangely for a comet, slowing down and speeding up unpredictably. While most research describes comets as dirty snowballs or icy dirtballs or even, more appetizing, deep-fried ice cream, it has long been suspected based on meteorite analysis that comets contain adenine as well as guanine."

"Adenine? Guanine?"

"Components of DNA and RNA." Cleona spread her napkin on her lap. The lights dimmed and elevator music softly wafted in. "There is a theory that comets carried all the water to earth that fills our oceans, and some scientists, including myself, think that comets and meteorites brought the components of life itself to our planet, that the amino acids that comprise proteins could be created by shock synthesis. Although we cannot exactly replicate the conditions of early earth in a lab setting, initial results have been promising."

"I read somewhere that comets were considered bad luck in ancient cultures." Amanda said.

"Especially in the Middle Ages. They were seen as omens of deaths of kings or noble men, of approaching catastrophes, or even, in alliance with the superticious beliefs of that time period, actual attacks by angels on earthlings. And in Norse culture, the sky was believed to be fashioned from the giant Ymir's skull, and comets were believed to be pieces of his skull fallen to earth."

"Cosmic dandruff," Zach muttered, and Amanda rolled her eyes again.

Cleona forged on. "Pieces of this so-called cosmic dandruff fluttered to earth and I believe this woman has found a specimen. I want to test it for organic molecules. The comet split once before and I tried to recover some samples in Antarctica but that mission was—unsuccessful."

"Big fucking deal," Zach commented. He had suddenly found his napkin very interesting. "Life is overrated."

"I wonder if that lady thought that too," Amanda said. "The lady that you—"

Zach shot her a deadly look.

Fortunately Emma brought their drinks and they sipped in silence. Amanda drank a bit too quickly and she had to ask for a refill by the time their soup arrived.

The next morning, Reginald was already dressed, hiking boots laced and sleeves folded up over his thin arms, and drinking coffee at 4:45. He was grateful for the coffee machine in the room since he was awake even before the most dedicated of hotel staff members. He had never needed a lot of sleep and as he grew older he needed even less. After a death sentence, every minute becomes precious, and Reginald preferred to spend his minutes awake.

The sky was beginning to lighten but Reginald took no notice. He was focused on creating a battle plan. A topographical map of the area was spread on the table in front of him, held down in one corner by his coffee cup. His ran his fingers along the map as if he could actually feel the mountains, like a blind man reading braille.

He would find Lucia the way he had found the enemy camps in Vietnam—logic and the process of elimination. He studied the map. She would have to be located near a source of water. He marked all the streams in the area with a blue highlighter pen.

She would also need to be near a good piece of flat ground for the farming or livestock that had probably once been her livelihood. He circled usable areas with a green highlighter pen.

She would need easy access to the village. He marked all the hiking paths with the orange highlighter. He did not use the pink pen. He disliked the color pink. It reminded him of (sunlight, flowers, women, love) he didn't know what but he didn't like it. Then he carefully capped the highlighters and stowed them in his breast pocket. The colors were as bright as children's auras he had seen on the playground three and ¾ blocks from his house on the 21st of December at 3:36 p.m.—a flash of fluorescent orange behind the slide, bright blue and green on a see-saw, a flaming yellow on a swing.

He forced his concentration back to the map. Every day was getting harder to focus and that scared him. The jungle of his memories bulged behind a flimsy curtain. He mustn't go off on tangents. It would be too easy to spend the rest of his life remembering the life he had already lived.

There were three likely areas where the colors intersected and he might find Lucia's cabin. He looked impatiently at his watch and sighed. It was still too early to set off. His cold coffee tasted like Vietnam tea again. In spite of himself, his thoughts broke loose again, drifting back to January 18, 1971.

It is she who will find you. That's what Private Miller had said with his last breath. But the dying soldier hadn't suggested that Reginald mount a search mission halfway around the world to find a woman he had never met. He also hoped to find hints of his father. Maybe he was on a wild goose chase.

"But she did find me," he said aloud. "She found me

first— in Dr. Nussbaum's waiting room right before I got my death sentence. All I have to do now is find her back."

He gave up on waiting for daylight and started to dress for walking in knee-deep snow. He figured that Lucia might be like him and have little use for sleep. He took his lucky crystal out of his pants pocket. He was nervous, and could use all the luck he could get. "You come from these mountains," he whispered to it. "Find your way home."

Cleona ventured out of the hotel at 7:10 in the morning after she had eaten breakfast in the dining room, thankfully alone. She surmised that Amanda was nursing a hangover and Zach was watching pornos on his portable communication device.

She gave herself a mental pat on the back for her performance last night. She wasn't very good at social encounters, but maybe she was improving. She had spent a whole evening in the company of other human beings. It was a start. Amanda and Zach were so emotionally crippled anyway they didn't have the inclination to notice that she, too, was damaged goods. That reminded her about Marc, her first attempt at a relationship. The relationship had been his idea, anyway. She strolled down the street, remembering.

July 19th, 2005

They had met because he wouldn't go away. He stood right in front of her presentation table, eyes drilling into her. She had shuttled her gaze from left to right, desperately hoping for someone else to approach her stand at the expo, admire her crystal displays, ask her questions about rocks. Anything to give her something else to pay attention to. But every time her gaze shifted, the man shifted as well.

The exhibition hall itself was a study in empty space. Borox, the sponsor, had decided to pair geology exhibits with astronomical ones, but apparently the combination that wasn't very popular at 9:30 in the morning. It was hard to tell if astronomy, geology, or the vacuum of space was supposed to be the focus. There were great gaps between the booths and the ceiling stretched 20 meters above their heads. The acoustics were odd, the sounds of footfalls and ripping of scotch tape were both magnified and muffled. There weren't many visitors yet, but there was this annoying man.

Cleona gave in and focused her full attention on him. He had eyes the color of clay and his thick brown hair had veins of silver running through it. Premature, Cleona guessed, maybe a twenty-two-year-old in a thirty-year-old`s body. He looked as though he hadn't shaved in five days, and Cleona guessed that he had done so on purpose. His nose was wide and his nostrils flared with mirth. "Can I help you?" she finally asked.

"That's a nice piece of crystal you got there." He pointed to one of her specimens. Some of the other exhibitors had stones mounted on velvet and other plush material. Cleona didn`t coddle her rocks. But she did label the displays with in her own handwriting, more even than her computer printer.

"It's Swiss mountain crystal. Fairly common in that region."

"Very well shaped." The man grinned and his clay eyes disappeared in happy wrinkles. Cleona had the feeling that he was trying to let her know something that had nothing to do with mountain crystal, but she didn't know what. "I like it."

"Yes, a near perfect hexagon."

"Can I take you out on a date?"

Cleona leaned forward. Had she misunderstood him? "It's July 19th, 2005."

He smiled. "No, I know what date it is. I'm asking you out. Some people from my department told me about this new restaurant and maybe you would like to try it out with me?"

Cleona looked around futilely, feeling like a lab rat in a cage looking down a needle. Suddenly she felt her pulse in her neck. O curse the waning interest of youth in science! There would be no rescue from this predicament. Most of the booths were empty and there were only a few visitors poking around, no one even close to her who could save her.

"Or do you have a boyfriend?"

"No, no," she stammered. "To what purpose?"

"What do you mean?"

"Why do you want to date me?"

"Well, to get to know each other better, of course. That's what people on dates do."

"I have never been on a date."

His jaw unhinged. "What? A beautiful girl like you? I can't believe that!"

"It's true." Cleona lifted her chin.

"Why not? Because you never wanted to?"

"I don't plan on having children. Hence, I don't need a partner. So, there is no reason to go out on a date." That was her killer statement, which was usually effective. The majority of her potential daters looked confused or hurt or even angry (one accused Cleona of thinking herself a class better than he was—she wasn't—just a class different) but they all slunk away in the end.

But this man didn't look upset. In fact, he grinned. "Look, I just asked you out on a date. I didn't ask to impregnate you."

"But isn't that the purpose of dating? Trying out potential partners?"

"Why don't you want children?" he countered.

"This is a question for people who know each other well," Cleona chided. She stepped back.

"Well, since you don't want to date me, I figured we could skip the whole getting-to-know-each-other bit and go directly into the awkward-questions part."

"I didn't say that I didn't want to date you." Cleona crossed her arms. "I simply stated that there is no reason to."

"Aha!" The man pounded the table so hard that all of her rocks jumped. "So, you might consider doing something which you wanted to do but for which you had no reason for doing?"

"I didn't say that I wanted to date you, either."

"But don't you think it's too big of a coincidence that destiny brought us here to this exhibition hall today of all days?" He waved his arms to encompass all the space. "It's not as if there are crowds straining at the doors. It's practically just you and me."

"I have a contract with Borax, not destiny. The definition of coincidence is two things that happen at the same time. Fate doesn't exist."

"What if I gave you a reason to want to date me? One that has nothing to do with children?"

Cleona folded her arms. "You could try."

"These—" he gestured to her display, "are all earthly rocks. I'm sure you know all about earthly rocks. But I could show you rocks from another world."

"Moon rocks?"

"Sure, among others. I'm Marc Hemmings, by the way. I'm an astronomer. My booth is over there."

"Well, Mr. Hemmings. I guess in that case I could just stroll over to your exhibit and see all your special rocks without having to date you." Cleona grinned.

"What's your name?"

Cleona pointed to her name tag.

"Cleona Skye. Well if that isn't a sign, I don't know what is. Skye? Sky?"

"I just told you what I thought about coincidences."

"Look, I want to share my passion with you."

"Is that another way of asking for a date?"

"About rocks, I mean. There are treasures and secrets in my rocks, I'm serious. I know you know all about reading stories from stones, but these are only short chapters in a mammoth epic. I have minerals that have been flying around the solar system since it was created, formed by processes we can only guess at. Did you ever realize that astronomy is the science of 'could be'? It 'could be' that dark energy exists, it 'could be' that the universe formed with The Big Bang. These rocks are history in solid form, but not just human history. I'm talking about the history of the universe. The history of everything. So many puzzles yet to be solved! Doesn't that sound interesting to you?"

Yes, it did. But she didn't want to admit it to this Marc Hemmings. She knew how to research; she had her own resources. "Thanks for the tip. Now if you will excuse me, I have to urinate. And I'm not going to wash my hands after I do it." She turned to walk away, deciding that it was worth leaving her precious stones unguarded just to get away from this man.

"Wait a minute!" He called to her retreating back. "Haven't you ever made a wish on a falling star?"

She froze. Yes, she had. The silver arch over her head, pointing west. And she had wished west. Her heart piggyback on a comet's tail to fly back where she came from, where it no longer smelt of burnt copper and rubber. To see those smiling eyes again. Where it smelt of lush gardens and hope. She turned back.

"I knew it!" His grin was adorable in triumph. "You did make a wish. What did you wish for?"

Her pulse throbbed in her neck again. "That's none of your business."

"Did you wish for children?"

"No!" She took a deep, shaky breath. "No. Of course not," she confirmed.

"Did it come true? Your wish?"

"No. And there's not even the most infinitesimal chance that it ever will."

"I'm sorry about that." He looked genuinely sad. "And still, you wished anyway." He placed his hands on the table leaned forward. "Cleona, I could show you something you have never seen before. If you go out with me, I will show it to you. You know, to make up for the wish that didn't come true. The one that got away."

"Alright," Cleona said. "I will go on a date with you. How does it work? What do I have to do?"

"You will? Really?" Marc smiled. "If you can wait a bit on going to the Ladies, I'll write down your address. Tell me when I should be there."

Cleona wrote neatly on a piece of paper and handed it to him. "Tomorrow. Eight o'clock," she said.

"Great! I'm looking forward to it. Just promise to wash your hands first." He winked.

Cleona had given her hands a hard scrubbing and then waited on her porch for Marc Hemmings. He screeched to the curb in a little royal blue Toyota that looked as though it had been rescued from the scrap metal pile. She walked up to the vehicle before he could get out, disinfected the handle and let herself in the rear of the car.

Marc looked at her in the rearview mirror and their eyes met. "Why are you sitting in the back seat?"

"It is the statistically safest place in a car." She fastened her seat belt.

"Well, then, I don't might playing chauffeur." He gripped the steering wheel. "Where to, Madame Skye?"

"This whole date thing was your idea. If you don't know where to take me, I can get out right now." She reached for the buckle.

He looked in the rearview mirror again and grinned. "Relax, Cleona Skye. I was only joking. I already reserved a table for us at the restaurant I told you about." He turned around in his seat so he could look at her. "I know this whole dating thing is new to you. Thanks for giving me a chance."

Cleona did relax then. A little. "What about this special thing you wanted to show me?"

"After dinner. I will take you there. I promise. It has to be dark," he added cryptically.

She observed his grip on the steering wheel, the slight movements of his fingertips, and concluded that he might be a good lover. Although Cleona had never had a date or a boyfriend, she had taken a couple lovers just so she could know what she was missing. Which, she had concluded, was not much.

Marc brought them safely to Chez Lumiere and he helped her out of the car, gripping her elbow, like a gentleman from another era. The lights in the parking lot were already on, bathing the cars in a strange glow.

She observed the guests in restaurant and concluded that they might be the only heterosexual couple. Huge palm trees scattered throughout the dining room lent an atmosphere of beach dining, and the ceiling was painted with a tacky rendition of a sunset by the beach. A plastic seagull swung above her head riding the waves of air conditioning. She couldn't shake the feeling that it might poop on her.

"What can I bring you?" Alexi, their server, asked.

"You have an interesting name," Cleona said. "Is it Russian?"

"My name is actually Alexa, but I go by Alexi."

"Wise choice. I'll have the Seaside salad and tap water, please," Cleona said.

"And I'll take the fish burger, a coke and a side of fries," Marc said. "By the way, do you know any jokes?"

"Did you hear about the new restaurant on the moon?" Alexi asked.

Marc shook his head, Cleona looked at her expectantly.

"The food is excellent, but there's no atmosphere."

Marc guffawed.

"Actually the moon does have atmosphere, a scant presence of gases totaling about 3×10 to the negative 15th power atm, so about 0.3 nPa, but it varies throughout the day." Cleona said.

"I'll be right back with your water." Alexi said.

Marc leaned in. "Did you mean an earth day or a lunar day?"

"What kind of astronomer are you? An earth day of course. The moon is gravitationally locked to earth so all lunar days are eternal. The moon has been experiencing the same day for millenia."

"I didn't know you were an astronomy expert." He grinned and Cleona felt something strange and unknown in her stomach—it pirouetted and leapt like a ballet dancer. Her cheeks grew hot. When Alexi finally brought her salad, Cleona concentrated on separating all the greens and vegetables into separate piles on her plate. She was aware of Marc watching her as she speared corn kernels with her fork and lifted them straight off the plate, making a right angle when she reached the level of her mouth.

"I never saw anyone eat that way before," he said.

She shrugged and shoveled in another forkful. "Are you a pain in the neck?"

"What?"

"Oh no, I didn't ask that right. I mean, do you ever have neck pain? From looking up all the time? That's what astronomers do, right?"

"Right. But I usually use a telescope. Still, it's not a comfortable position for the human body to twist into for long periods of time."

Cleona sighed and examined her fingers. "I wish I could get the dirt out from under my fingernails. I scrub and scrub but I can never quite manage to get all of it. That's an occupational hazard, I guess. Just like you and your telescope yoga."

He grinned around a mouthful of fish sandwich and her heart hammered out ten jumping jacks. "Telescope yoga. I like that. Isn't it strange that your job is looking down and mine is looking up?"

"Your job is dreaming and guessing. You said yourself that astronomy is the science of possibilities. I don't know how you can tolerate that. I prefer to deal in things that are real." She held up her fingers for him to examine. "Real grit from real rocks. You will never get stardust under your fingernails."

"You know as well as I do that my fingernails are stardust, my heart and my lungs and yours as well and everything around us is all stardust."

She shook her head. "You know what I mean."

"But even besides that, the Late Heavy Bombardment ended 3.8 billion years ago, but meteors are still falling to earth. So the stars are still falling to us. As a matter of fact, an average of 60 tons of meteoritic dust falls to earth every single day, which is the weight equivalent to forty hippopotamuses."

"Hippopotami," Cleona corrected.

He looked at her plate. "Are you finished?"

Cleona looked down and realized that her salad was gone. She wasn't even aware that she had eaten it.

Marc signaled Alexi for the bill that she delivered with overtones of relief. "C'mon." He laid some dollars on the table and stood up. "And I will show you what I promised."

The road up to the Griffith Observatory was long and winding. Marc pulled over in a parking area and lifted a telescope out of his trunk. "Come with me. If you dare." He wiggled his eyebrows at her and she followed him away from the streetlights. "Here." He handed her a flashlight with a red beam. "Red light is better for your night vision."

"Where are we going? I thought you were going to show me something."

"I am! But we will need the telescope to see it."

She had never been in the woods at night. This isn't the most intelligent thing I've ever done, she thought as she followed this stranger deeper into the forest. But she wasn't afraid. He set up his telescope in a clearing and took a few minutes to find a celestial object and capture it in focus. Cleona didn't speak. She watched how his fingers manipulated the focus knob and wondered again if he would be a good lover.

He nodded, satisfied. "Come and have a look, then."

She bent down, practicing a bit of telescope yoga herself, and squinted into the lens. At first the night sky and stars appeared swimmy but she blinked and an object came into focus. It was long and thin and red and looked like a flying cigar. She couldn't be certain but it seemed to be rotating.

"I give up. What is that?"

Marc put his hand on her shoulder, causing a low grade electrical buzz under her skin. "No one knows for sure. It's called Recce's comet, but no one is sure yet what it actually is. It is estimated to be stone instead of ice. Its origin is outside the solar system. And it did something really weird as it slingshot around the sun. Something that doesn't make any sense considering Einstein's theory or any theory at all for that matter."

Cleona looked at him. "Why? What did it do?"

"Why, it slowed down. Markedly as it passed earth. As if it were taking a good look at us."

Cleona looked back through the eyepiece just as Recce's Comet rolled out of her vision. She scrambled to adjust the telescope to keep it in her view. Something sparked inside her, a sense of purpose. "What would I have to do to get a sample of that?" She straightened up.

"Fly," Marc answered, and swept her into his arms.

Although she pointedly did not believe in coincidences, she found it ironic that her thoughts of Marc had brought her to a graveyard. But it wasn't an ordinary cemetery. The bones buried below the stone markers were those of adventurers—mountain climbers who had lost their lives while scaling the Matterhorn. One of the gravestones had hiking boots hanging from it's cross, another had poles leaning against it, another bits of rope scattered on top. Fresh flowers were lying on the snow in front of one of the markers and a candle was flickering in a red tube although the person who was buried there died 73 years ago. Then there was a plain grave marker with no flowers, candles or decorations that made her feel sad—William Patterson, born April 17, 1920, died June 26, 1948. Cleona gave the dead a brief nod of respect. While she had negative desire to climb a mountain, she could understand how people could be so obsessed with a challenge that it destroyed them in the end. Her obsession with Recce's comet had begun over ten years ago and had taken over her life. It had even almost brought her death in Antarctica.

She left the cemetery and wandered back up to the church square. A marker on the side of the street, fortunately free of snow, grabbed her attention. It was a plaque commemorating a time capsule that had been buried last year containing wishes from native third grade children for their beloved Zermatt. It was scheduled to be unearthed and examined in fifty years. "Ha," Cleona scoffed to herself. "Wishes are best left buried."

The streets of Zermatt were just waking up with electric cars making deliveries and employees going to work. The tourists, even the early skiers, weren't stirring yet. It was the perfect time to search for Lucia, and leave shattered thoughts of the past behind her.

Cleo had done her homework. She had already tried googling Lucia's address and phone number from Mexico but there was nothing listed. However she did discover that Zurbriggen was a popular name in the area. She had cold-called several of them to ask about the mysterious Lucia, but only one of them spoke English—one Imogene Zurbriggen. "I tink she liwe in cabin ower willage," Imogene had said. German speakers had difficulty with the 'th' and 'v' sounds. After translation, Cleo thought that description fit well with the photo she had clipped from the magazine.

As she paced the square in front of the church and museum searching for an unobstructed view of the mountains, she felt that the snowdrifts lining the curbs seemed to be closing in on her like white monsters slouching against the street. She stuck to the middle of the square, the maximum distance away from the snow beasts.

"Hey lady, you want kebab?" A greasy woman called out from behind Barb's Sausage Stand.

For breakfast? Cleona thought. "No thank you."

To keep herself from thinking about the snow, she dove into her scientist mode and studied her environment. Observation: The indigenous people, the ones delivering cases of soda and fresh fruit to the hotels and hawking kebabs at seven thirty in the morning, looked scruffier than the soft-looking tourists. More hardy. But not buried under layers of clothes like the scientists in Antarctica. They had been bundled up in their bright red down jackets and sporting sunglasses that covered half their faces. The residents of Zermatt were different, they wore drab, frayed garments—olive green jackets and prison blue pants. Their skin had toughened up over generations so that one layer of clothing might be enough and their eyes were slits from squinting so much. She smiled at her own prowess. Charles Darwin would have appreciated her evolutionary conclusions, and she was able to keep her breathing rate regular, not thinking about the snow.

As she left the square and walked up the street, the natives flocked back into whatever caves they had emerged from and the tourists in colorful ski jackets gushed from their luxury apartments and hotels, flocking in the direction of the ski lift.

Cleo found another square next to a field. It had an adequate view of the Matterhorn and the mountains surrounding the village. She turned around slowly, surveying the landscape. It was hard to tell where Lucia's cabin could be. The mountainsides were dotted with small sheds, probably for storing hay or live-stock. It was hard to spot a cabin among these, but she did see where an avalanche had tumbled down. Recently, by the looks of it. Cleo shuddered as she tried to shove her terror to the side.

She took the folded picture out of her pocket. Don't think about the avalanche. Concentrate on your goal. Lucia Zurbriggen was holding the meteorite. She was smiling, and to Cleo she looked like a wise woman from a fairy tale. Too bad Cleo didn't believe in fairy tales, or she could just follow a trail of breadcrumbs or peek into a crystal ball to find her. Lucia was stand-ing in a doorway, presumably her own. The moun-tains in the background could be any of the moun-tains around here.

But there was a dog in the picture, looking up lov-ingly at Lucia. Its coat was shiny, its teeth gleamed, its tongue rosy pink.

Such a dog was well cared for. That meant visits to the vet. Cleona pulled out her smart phone and googled vets in the area. There was only one. Cleo set off in the opposite direction of the skiiers, dodging their shouldered skis while feeling a bit like a salmon swimming upstream.

At an easy ramble, with stops to poke in posh stores and drink a frothy milk-coffee and nibble a crois-sant, it would take a couple of hours to ramble from one end of Zermatt to the other. For a scientist on a mission it took 40 minutes. Cleo passed by choco-late shops, bakeries, quaint drugstores specializing in sun block and sports balm and myriad clothing stores with mannequins dressed in vibrant snowsuits with fake fur trim that cost thousands of dollars. The only souvenir she wanted was a chunk of outer space.

The vet was on the outskirts of town near the big parking garage where the tourists had to deposit their SUVs and other gas guzzlers. Cleona identified the building by a picture of a cuddly puppy and kitten on the door.

The inside of the office was basic and functional. It was an apartment converted into a practice and the waiting room was the former living room. Cleona could tell by the light-color television shape against the grey wall. The reception area smelled of dry dog food, which was sold from buckets lined up against the wall.

"Can I help you?" the bright receptionist asked in German. She looked a bit puzzled at Cleona's lack of pet. "Are you lost?" she asked in English.

"I am looking for a dog. Actually the owner of a dog." She pulled out the magazine article to show the receptionist.

She smiled. "Ja, tat's Sparky und Lucia."

"Can you tell me where they live?"

The bright sun of her face was crossed by a cloud. "Wat do you need tat for?"

"I wanted to ask her where she got her dog. I used to have one like that when I was a little girl and I was interested in getting another one."

"Oh, we adwise people not to do tat. It honor not the memory of they original pet."

"I see." Cleo forced herself to look miserable. Being

an actress was difficult for her, but when the Nobel Prize was at stake she could pull off an Oscar-winning performance. "It's just that, you know, Bella was such a part of our family. We loved her so much, and that love never died, even when she did. When I saw this picture in a magazine it brought it all back. I'm sure you love animals too?"

"Oh ja!" the receptionist said. "Our famwily had a golden retriewer like Sparky when I was growing up." She studied Cleo. "I suppose it ok. Miss Lucia don't have fwiends still living and I know not where she get her dog, but you ask her yourself." She pointed outside. "Miss Lucia liwes behind the Weisshorn. When my mom was young the Zurbriggens have restaurant tere, for hikers and climbers of Matterhorn. Go this way, always Matterhorn in front of you. Tose old signs are still tere, like a secret code fro trail. Follow the yellow arrows with star on dem. They call restaurant 'Stern', tat's German for 'star'."

"Thank you so much! You've been a big help. I'm sure Bella can rest easy in her doggie grave now. Thank you!" Cleo fled the vet's office and the perky receptionist's confused look.

It was warming up, a strange kind of warm where it was still freezing but the raw sun made it seem hot. Her breath was no longer visible in front of her face. It was a good day for hiking, if she could ignore the megatons of snow that surrounded her.

Chapter 6

Astra Nova Berkovitz was at her desk in the process of filling out the forms (in triplicate) to have her last name changed when a photo in the newspaper lying next to her caught her attention. She threw in her breath with a hiss. Six days ago she had been awakened by the sound like a freight train plowing through the night sky. Now she knew what it had been. A meteorite! And it had landed just over the mountain.

An idea popped into her head.

"Rufus! Get in here!"

Her brother stumbled in, somehow managing to trip over his own feet. He grabbed the doorway for support. "What's wrong, Astra?"

"How old is this newspaper?"

"I don't know, sister heart. Is there a date on it?"

She kept her gaze averted from the drool hanging from his lip. It wasn't his fault that their parents were the first test candidates for LSD, but it wasn't her fault either. It was as if the drug had altered her parents' genetic makeup, and stolen more than a few IQ points from her brother. But since their parents had died, it became her problem, despite the fact that she hadn't even been born when her parents had taken the drug.

"The part with the date is missing," she said. A cloud of worry passed over Rufus' face. "No problem, brother. I can figure it out."

Their parents had died in a hiking accident when she was ten and Rufus was thirteen, and she had been looking after him ever since then. Their grandmother had still been alive and assumed the legal role as guardian, and her social security checks had kept them in groceries, but she was about all she was able to do in way of raising them. She did little more than rock back and forth in her rocking chair. On the porch in summer, in the living room in winter. Their neighbors (if you could call them that, they lived so far away) had offered the occasional casserole and lecture about the importance of schooling. Astra gave them a pert nod, thanked them for the casserole, and ignored their advice.

Eventually she started telling the neighbors that the mountain took care of them—to make up for killing their parents. The casseroles stopped coming after that.

Their grandmother had been fanatically superstitious and deeply religious. Somehow these two factors warped together in her head as she rocked back and forth and she became convinced that Astra, with her white blonde hair and blue eyes, was the reincarnation of a goddess. She sent Astra's picture to some strange magazines containing articles rife with prophecies and misspellings. Astra had been ordained High Priestess of The Children of the Snowflake (who worshiped snow) by a mail order course and opened their home (a falling-apart youth hostel) to her followers. Her grandmother had died two years ago, suffering from dementia and unable to string words together to make a sentence, but Astra knew enough by then to take over the 'business'. She applied Children of the Snowflake for church tax status. She had been looking after her brother for her entire life, and now she was looking after her Children too, the average age of the 'children' being 64.

You should be thankful, she scolded herself as she looked at her brother. All you ended up with was the funny name. He was unfortunate enough to get swatted by the stupid stick. But in appearance he was just as angelic as she was. Perhaps even more so with his child-like glow and silver drool—like a melting halo, she thought.

She scanned the article again. Now and then her position as High Priestess entailed that she had to make predictions or come up with quests to keep the Children occupied, something more interesting than knitting booties for charity. That was all part of the church deal.

"Call the clan together, brother. The object for our quest has been revealed to me in a vision. We will make a great pilgrimage, and fortunately the object of desire had the decency to land close to us, so we don't have to even 'pilgrim' very far!" This was fortunate, she thought, because she probably could convince her congregation to walk over the mountain but not to journey to the Sea of Galilee, for example. I should have had myself listed as a nursing home rather than a church, Astra thought. I might get even more of a tax break! Oh well, maybe next year.

She pushed the photo across the desk to him. He

couldn't read, but he was able to make simple deductions from pictures. "Here, look. It says her name is Lucia Zurbriggen from Zermatt. She has the piece of God's soul that ripped through my dreams a couple weeks ago. We shall pay a visit to this woman!"

Rufus glowed. "What a good idea, Sisterheart!" Then his grin faltered. "What makes you think that God's soul comes in solid form?"

Astra smiled ruefully. Maybe he wasn't as dumb as he looked.

It was high noon but there was far too much snow for a shootout in the Wild West. Reginald noted with a shiver that the camouflage jacket which had kept him warm when he was 40 years old did not help him at 76. Yet he was sweating. The weather was a queer mix of warmth from the sun (he was closer to it now than in the Pennsylvania lowlands) and freezing— the temperature lay at a crisp minus 11 Celsius. He kept trudging along but wasn't sure that he was going the correct way because there was no path to follow, just colored sticks in the snow. He assumed he was on the right track as he followed the rough wooden posts curving over the slope. The sky was too bright to look at and the snow reflected the brilliance. Reginald's eyes ached. He knew that blue eyes were more sensitive to the sun than darker ones. He concentrated on not letting the migraine in as he soldiered on. At least his boots were good. They hugged his thin calves and protected him from the snow.

There were no other people out here, no auras, no

noise. Reginald was thankful for that. Ever since October 3rd at 9:26 a.m. he had suffered hallucinations. He remembered that day as he matched through the drifts half a world away.

October 3rd, 2015 9:15 a.m.

He had been presiding over court, filling in for Judge Booker. Judge Raymond Booker was ill with something serious on indefinite leave. Reginald hadn't asked what. He hadn't wanted to know.

He had been peering down at the defendant in front of him. The docket stated that she was sixteen-years-old but it was hard to tell her age under all that black eyeliner. She was on the pudgy side and had a face made for chewing gum. She reminded him of Veronica Fulwright whom he had sentenced to six months probation on March 16th 1982 at 11:56 a.m., just before lunchtime. On that day he had eaten a ham sandwich for lunch with too much mustard slathered on it and an especially sour pickle slipped inside. He glanced at the docket. Cheyenne, the defendant's name was Cheyenne Peterson, not Veronica Fulwright. Concentrate. Concentrate. He leveled his gaze at her. "Do you have anything to say in your defense?"

Reginald hadn't tried or sentenced a shoplifter in a long time. Judge Booker handled misdemeanors and family cases. But Judge Booker might never come back, the courtroom atmosphere was heavy with his absence. Clearing throats and coughs seemed extra loud.

Cheyenne's eyes were almost lost in the pudginess of her cheeks. "Not really." The girl's public defender was checking her fingernails, not interested in her client at all.

The state attorney, who had rested two minutes and forty-three seconds ago, was ruffling through some papers, probably preparing for his next case. The plaintiff, the owner of the jewelry store, had already left. It seemed as if all parties were ready to move on to the next thing.

Except Reginald. "Young lady, can you tell me why you stole the necklace?"

Cheyenne shrugged. "I wanted it, but I didn't have the money to pay for it."

"But you do know that stealing is illegal?"

She shrugged again.

"And it didn't matter to you?"

"Not really."

"Do you regret your actions?"

"Yeah. I got arrested and I didn't even get to keep the necklace."

Reginald looked at the evidence photo. The security guard had found the necklace in Cheyenne's purse. The charm was a silver dolphin, leaping through the air.

"Do you like dolphins?"

Cheyenne shifted uncomfortably. "Yeah."

Reginald glanced around the courtroom. The public's benches were empty except for a drunk man snoring with his mouth open. "Where are your parents?"

"I'm in a foster home."

"Why? Didn't your parents love you?"

Cheyenne looked at her lawyer for help. At this last question the public defender slapped the table and shouted "Objection!"

"You can't object you ridiculous woman," Reginald said. "I am the judge."

The public defender reddened. "Please accept my apologies Judge Booker. Is Your Honor ready to sentence my client?"

"I am Judge Patterson, Judge Booker is on leave. Don't you read your own dockets? You should know in front of whom you are appearing. And no I am not ready to hand down my sentence." He looked at Cheyenne again. "Who named you?"

"What?" She had started to chew imaginary gum, out of nervousness.

"Who gave you the name Cheyenne?"

"My Dad picked it out."

"Why?"

"I guess he just liked that name."

"It's a beautiful name. Why isn't your Dad here, Cheyenne?"

"I—I don't know."

"Where is your Dad, Cheyenne?"

"I don't know that either."

"Objection!" This time the state attorney was on his feet. "Your Honor, with all due respect, what does Cheyenne Peterson's father have to do with this case?"

"Everything!" boomed Reginald. "Where is he? Who raised this young lady? Why couldn't she wish for a dolphin necklace on her birthday and her father surprise her with it? Did she even have a cake? Did she even—" Suddenly he stopped. Everyone was looking at him. The two lawyers were wide-eyed, and Cheyenne's mouth had dropped open. Daphne, the court reporter, had stopped typing. Even the drunk at the back of the gallery had regained consciousness and was staring at him.

"Judge Patterson, is everything all right?" Daphne asked.

Reginald blinked and suddenly the room was flooded with color. Every person had a different hue ... the state's attorney had a crimson, Cheyenne had salmon pink. The Public Defender had teal and Daphne had an efficient blue. The drunk in the back had a sickly olive green. All the colors rose up in the room and intermingled with each other. Reginald gaped. The Northern Lights had invaded Courtroom Number 5.

"Judge Patterson?" Daphne asked again.

Reginald blinked and all the colors vanished.

And that's when Reginald realized that he had best see a doctor.

*

A tiled roof peaked over the rise, snapping him out of his reverie. He had to be so careful not to get lost in the land of his infinite memory. If he concentrated he could remember everything about Courtroom Number 5, from the cracks in the walls to how many gemstones had been in the ring Daphne was wearing. Not real diamonds, of course. No one could afford real diamonds on a court stenographers salary. Reginald forced himself to concentrate on walking, rounding the path with determination—almost, but not quite, marching. The mountains in front of him were configured exactly like the photograph. The answers he needed lay in that house—he was sure of it.

He took the picture of his father out of his pocket and studied it. He was here. Man had a tendency to change his environment, but nature endured. The mountains were in the exact same spots as they were sixty years ago. The glaciers had ebbed back of course, climate change, but Reginald was experiencing the same view from the same spot as his father had before him. He turned around slowly, noting the jagged outline of the peaks, threatening to tear open the sky. The brightness of the sun/snow/sky made his eyes ache. His father was the one hole in his memory—he could barely recall his smile, the colors in his iris, his laugh, the jokes he used to tell. Reginald had the feeling his mind monkey had erased his father on purpose. Some memories were too painful to relive. He turned towards the cabin.

It was built from chunks of grey rocks with a bluish tinge. It stuck out of the snow like a defiant stone box. The wooden door had long cracks that ran from top to bottom and were big enough to stick a finger in. Reginald knocked on it.

The door opened a couple inches. An eye peaked out. The brow above wrinkled. "Was wollen Sie?"

Reginald inhaled deeply. He hadn't planned his opening statement. He hadn't been prepared for anything at all. He had come here following a wisp of a dream and a need, like a plant, to grow towards the light.

She opened the door a bit wider.

"Ma'am, you don't know me."

Lucia sighed. "I losing my memory. I know not who I know and who I know not." Her powder blue aura was streaked with gold.

Reginald smiled. "Well, I have enough memories to share with you if you want. A lifetime's worth. Every detail."

"No, no thank you. I chose it— I want forget things. Don't know why anymore. Don't remember." She heaved another grand sigh.

"Did it begin after you found the meteorite?"

Her eyes narrowed.

"How do you know I found meteorite?" Her aura turned an impertinent royal blue. "Who are you? You come for meteorite?"

"No I'm not here for the meteorite. My name is Reginald Patterson. I saw your picture in the newspaper. And on the Internet."

"The internet? What you say." She smiled again, the sun coming from behind a cloud and her aura softened to baby blue again. "Am I famous?"

Reginald grinned. "I guess so. I saw your picture while I was in Pennsylvania."

"Transylvania? I never go to Romania before. I never left these mountains."

Reginald grinned and decided that it was too much trouble to correct her.

Her dog appeared at the door and she scratched absently between his ears. "What you need here, Mr. Patterson?"

"Please call me Reginald. Actually, I'm not really sure why I'm here."

Lucia's eyes gleamed with good humor. "Folks don't come here on accident, Mr. Reginald. Not like on the Autobahn." She looked him up and down. "I live alone. Not many visitors. Don't know people so well. My dog, Sparky, he feels things about people. He says you are all right because he don't bite off your fingers. You want to come in out of the cold, Mr. Reginald?"

Come in out of the cold. Reginald smiled. It was actually only pseudo cold, but those words made his heart leap. "Yes, Miss Lucia. I would like that very much."

She and Sparky moved aside to let him in. He stamped the snow from his boots. It was dark inside the little cabin, and his eyes adjusted slowly.

"You speak English very well," Reginald said. "Did you learn it in school?"

"I don't remember," Lucia said. She gestured to the one chair at her dining room table. There weren't any other chairs for guests. Reginald surveyed the room with reconnaissance eyes. It was rudimentary here—no pictures on the wall, no souvenirs or knick-knacks on the shelves. Reginald felt completely at home.

"No, Miss Lucia. I insist. You take the chair. I'll stand."

Lucia poured him a cup from whatever liquid she had on the stove and smiled. "No worries. I got twenty-three chairs on my porch. Don't know why anymore. Why I have so much chairs. But one is for you. You can get it, maybe? Then we both can sit."

"Of course." The porch was attached to the main house. There was a roof overhead, but the snow had blown in anyway, covering the floor of the porch. Reginald located the chairs under a tarp and lugged one in. Lucia was waiting for him at the table. She smiled as he sat down and pushed over a cup of whatever.

"So, tell me now why really you are here."

"I saw your picture while I was in the waiting room of my doctor's office. In Pennsylvania." Reginald took a sip of his drink. It tasted like burnt water. "I had the strong feeling that I was supposed to find you, although I cannot say why. I was a soldier, Miss Lucia, a colonel in the US Army. I am not a man given to flights of fancy. I found a picture of my father, while he was traveling in Europe, where he was standing near your house. I was hoping maybe you knew something about him."

"Can't remember much about my life, don't know what to tell you," Lucia answered. "Just something about wolves. There used to be wolves in the mountains. Does that mean something?"

"No idea." He held up his lucky crystal. "Do you recognize this?"

She took it out of his hand and held it up to the light to examine it. Rainbows flickered on the walls. "This is Bergkrystal, comes from here. These mountains are filled with crystal. And wolves. There used to be wolves."

"It was given to me in the war," Reginald continued, determined not to get sidetracked by wolves. "My father's name was William Patterson. Does that ring any bells? Maybe your parents knew him?"

"Maybe. Maybe not. Don't remember a William from Transylvania. Don't even remember my own mother, how she looked."

"Do you have a picture of her?"

Lucia brightened. "Maybe!" She rose and started rummaging around in an old sideboard. "This drawer's big mess! I don't remember if I clean it. Ever. Oh." She pulled out a tiny yellow infants's jumper. "What this?" She held it out to Reginald.

"Looks like clothes for a baby. Did you have any children, Lucia?"

"No. No I never." Her face wrinkled as if she wanted to throw the little jumper far away but she roughly folded it instead and used it to wipe the sideboard. She turned to Reginald. "What was I doing?"

"Looking for a picture of your mother," Reginald reminded her gently.

"Aha!" She looked up at him and smiled, flashing a picture. She drew her chair closer to him, smelling of spring rain and cabbage, and showed him the photograph.

It was old and yellowing, a woman with dark skin in a bonnet and a rotund man next to her leaning on a shovel and chewing on a piece of grass. "This my mother! Her name is—" Lucia stopped short, looking horrified.

"Yes?"

"I don't remember," she whispered.

Her distress distressed Reginald. "And the man? Is that your father?"

"No, no." she shook her head. "That is my uncle, Uncle Bruno." She smiled at him triumphantly. "My mother was his sister, yes, my mother's name is Hannelore!" Suddenly her smile faded. "You're bleeding." Her voice was curiously flat.

"What—?" Reginald reached up touched his upper lip and he felt the wetness. He pulled his fingers away bloody. He felt fat drops plunk out of his nose down his face. He grabbed his glove from the table and held it under his nose. Lucia fetched two towels, soaking one of them with water. She placed the wet one the back of his neck.

"Ah that's cold!"

She laughed. "Normal temperature here, but make bleeding stop. Here." She gently moved the glove away and put the dry towel under his nose.

Reginald looked at his own fingers, horrified. "That's never happened before." He couldn't keep the fear out of his towel-muffled voice.

Lucia smiled at him. "It nosebleed. It not end of the world. When mountain is high, nose is bleeding." Lucia's aura blinked back into Reginald's view. It was still baby blue and light gold, and she appeared to have a halo over her head.

Sparky lumbered over and lay at Reginald's feet.

"Could I—could I just stay here until it stops?"

"Of course." She squeezed his hand. "Reginald, why you alone? You had wife?"

Reginald gave her a little smile, shook his head and closed his eyes. His head felt a little swimmy. This is what death must be like, he thought. It will just come to me, and I can do nothing to stop it. And no wet towel will keep it at bay.

"Keep holding towel." He heard Lucia's voice from far away.

He nodded, keeping one hand on the cold towel on his neck and the other jammed on his nose. He had never felt so damn old and so vulnerable.

Then he felt her hand circle his wrist. He opened his eyes. "It stopped now? We look." He allowed her to take the towel away slowly. "There. Is better. You all right?"

Reginald stood up quickly and spilled his tea, coffee, whatever it was. "Thank you very much for your hospitality, Miss Lucia. I must be going now." He zipped up his jacket and pulled on his blood-damp glove. Sparky grunted and strolled over to the edge of the fireplace, where he collapsed in a fluffy heap.

"Wait! No hurry, Mr. Reginald! No run off. I have time—"

"The problem is, I don't." He bustled out the door. She hurried to the doorway to watch him scuttle down the path.

"Well, that was odd." She reached down to stroke her dog, reverting to German. "What a strange man.

Wonder what he wanted. Did he even tell me? Did I forget that too?"

She went back inside and noticed something gleaming on her table, glowing in the morning sun. She picked it up. His piece of mountain crystal. She slipped it into the pocket of her apron and hurried to the doorway, hoping to call him back.

But he was gone as if the mountain had swallowed him.

Cleona was struggling to hike up the mountain. She was relatively fit but the air was thin, the slope was steep and the snow was deep. Her panic kept her lungs in a vice and only shallow breaths were possible. She was trying not to think about the tons of snow surrounding her, imagining instead how the meteorite would feel in her hands. But the more she tried not to think about Antarctica, the more it haunted her. The achromatic tundra of Antarctica existed inside her now. An expansive reach of infinite snow, heartless and unforgiving. Ted's warning echoed in her head as she hiked up the mountain.

January 17th 2007

"Don't go over there," Ted had said. His voice had crackled over the receiver, built into Cleo's helmet.

There had been five of them in the scout group, Cleo was the only geologist. They were crossing the bleak Antarctic tundra on powerful snowmobiles, on the way back to camp. Cleo had stopped and the rest of them pulled even with her.

The helmets were fitted with both receivers and microphones, but Ted only used the microphone part and he preferred that the rest of them only used the receivers. He had some sort of military background; he had a voice used to giving commands. He raised his arm indicating some hills in the distance.

Cleo pointed in the same direction. "I see black spots over there. They could be meteors! Can't we go over and check them out?"

Ted looked at his wrist. He could probably see his watch through his jacket using his X-Ray vision. "Base said the storm is on its way. We have to get back to camp."

"But those rocks aren't far away! Can't we just go have a quick look?"

Ted shook his head. "You know as well as I do that it's not just a matter of 'a quick look'. We would have to photograph and triangulate the location before we harvest any meteorites. That takes time. Time we don't have." His helmet turned away from her. "Besides distances are different out here. Those rocks are farther away than you think."

The others bobbed their heads. She knew they were already annoyed with her, two meteorologists and two biologists, tired of stopping every time Cleo spotted something dark in the snow, helping her take all her measurements and notes when they had actually come to Antarctica to take ice core samples.

But it was her day. She had spent yesterday drilling

thick icicles for them. Now it was her turn, and her turn was almost over. Figures that the storm had to pick this day to come. Rage bubbled up inside her. "I didn't come all the way to Antarctica, getting seasick and throwing up over the railing of that God-forsaken ship the entire trip so I could ride around with you freaks on snowmobiles drilling pointlessly deep holes into ice! I came here to collect meteorites! If the weather is as bad as you are saying, they could be covered tomorrow!"

"I am the senior advisor." Ted's voice was tight. She knew that he had wanted to insert 'officer' instead of 'advisor' but it didn't matter because she was a civilian who didn't give a blow in a methane gas vent about hierarchy. "I've been on this continent for six months straight now. I know the weather patterns. Every second we discuss your temper tantrum here is a second more that we are in danger. Everyone keep following me back to the camp. That includes you, Miss Skye."

"Doctor Skye," Cleona corrected, although they had been on a first name basis since Day One.

Ted sped forward, giving no indication that he had heard her. The others following him like baby ducks, except ducks on snowmobiles instead of flippers. Cleo's head was so hot she was afraid that it was going to explode inside her helmet, but she followed them anyway.

Base camp was located tantalizingly close to where the Wilkes' Crater was reported to be. Because it was buried under tons of ice mass, no amount of geologist's drilling would confirm or deny the crater's existence. It was only recognizable from space. Marc had often commented that Cleona was drawn to the scars of the earth. Maybe because of her own scars. But she wasn't here to investigate Wilkes' Crater. She was here to finally collect her prize and satisfy that longing that had begun a year and a half ago—for meteorites fallen from Recce's Comet. For pieces from another world. She would be the first human being to hold a rock in her hand from outside the solar system.

It was an endless afternoon back at camp. The scientists started a penny poker game and discussed their families between hands, comparing baby pictures as the storm shrieked outside. Cleona stewed in her frustration. The fact that Ted had been right about the weather didn't help her mood at all. No one asked her to join the game. No one asked her if she had any baby pictures. No one was speaking to her. Even Cindy, a meteorologist with whom she had sort of bonded, being that they were the only two females on the mission, was focusing all her attention on her poker cards so she wouldn't have to look at Cleo. Being excluded from a group didn't really bother Cleo, being adopted had helped prepare her for that. Cleo played with her porridge at dinner, lifting it up with her spoon and dumping it back into her bowl. She excused herself early, retiring to the room she shared with Cindy. She stared at the ceiling for a few hours until she heard Cindy come in. Cindy went to bed without saying a word, and soon her breaths were long and even.

Cleo couldn't sleep. She rolled from one side of the bed to the other, which wasn't very far and rather difficult given that the cot was only a couple inches wider than she was. The views weren't very exciting—Cindy's blanketed back or the window with the outside floodlight shining through. There were no curtains, it seemed no one in Antarctica was concerned about homey touches.

Cindy's blanketed back, the window. The ceiling as alternative. When she closed her eyes meteors streaked across the backs of her eyelids. The idea of those meteorites she had seen wouldn't leave her alone. What if those were the ones she was searching for—remnants of Recce with organic molecules? Because that's the way it always was, wasn't it? The meteorites would be buried with snow tonight and in five years a new team would be here and the wind would blow a different way, freeing the meteorites again. The future team would recover them and get all the credit. The meteorite game was all about luck. Luck and courage.

Cleona hadn't been lucky today. But fortunately she had the courage (or the fearlessness) to make up for any lack of luck she might experience.

She sat up and threw the blanket to the floor. It was all a matter of scientific method, she reassured herself as she slipped on her thermal leggings. She used the scientific method as a way of working through difficult problems, as a framework of structure and logic, and as a way to keep chaos at bay.

First step .... ask a question. Were those meteors the

ones she was looking for, the ones that contained organic molecules?

Second step ... .background research. She could already check that one off, she had made herself an expert in meteorites. She ate, drank and slept meteorites since she met Marc, and topped it off with a PhD in Geology plus fifteen years field experience. A geyser on Recce had sent meteors tumbling toward earth at a trajectory that predicted landfall in Wilkes' Land, Antarctica, exactly where she had journeyed to. What were the chances that she would ever make it back here again?

Third step ... construction of a hypothesis. Those meteorites were the ones from Recce and contained organic molecules because they are the ones she hadn't examined yet, so tantalizingly out of reach. It was oh-so-logical, that what Cleona couldn't get her hands on was exactly what she was looking for. Hadn't it always been that way?

Fourth step ... test with an experiment. Elementary, dear Watson. One needed the meteorites for that. So in order to fulfill the fourth step she had to get those rocks.

But there were no empty slots in the scientific method, or the rational known universe for that matter, to take into account the brutality of the Antarctic night.

The snowmobiles were kept in a heated garage but the door wasn't locked. There were no burglars in Antarctica. No curtains, no crime, no prisons. The perfect society, a frozen utopia. That appealed to

Cleo. Only people like imperious Ted and insensate Cindy spoiled it.

She packed herself into the bulky red jacket and snow pants, specially designed for Antarctica. Its bulk made Cleo nearly as wide as she was tall, but the jacket wasn't any heavier than her winter coat back home. The window served as a mirror at night. Cleona was almost amused at the sight of herself. Her sleek oriental features were better suited to a kimono or a lab coat. She looked like the jolly red Michelin Man. She donned her helmet. She could be anyone in this outfit—Ted, Cindy, Bigfoot, anonymous. It was the uniform of desolate country.

She pressed the button to open the garage door and Antarctica roared in. Cleo lowered the helmet shield over her face but Antarctica still managed to creep in through the cracks on the sides, freezing tiny hairs on her face that she hadn't known existed. She mounted Ted's snowmobile. The key was in the ignition. It rumbled to life, the motor grinding like a chainsaw. She was becoming adept at driving snowmobiles, but it was a skill she did not intend to use anywhere once she left Antarctica. She maneuvered the machine out of the garage, glancing at the door in her rearview mirror. No one was following her. She knew that it would shut automatically in three minutes.

It was like driving on the dark side of Pluto. Her daytime field trips had not prepared her for the fierceness of an Antarctic storm at night.

Antarctica was the last frontier on earth, so hostile that no one chose to live there voluntarily. There was a one year cap on residencies in Antarctica, it was whispered after a year that people started the descent into madness. At night the landscape was completely alien. Here hell had frozen over, and maybe all the monsters and demons had come with it. The snow-mobile's headlamp was pathetic against the flurried darkness, and Cleo imagined she caught impressions of creatures just outside the circle of light. She tried to take comfort in the beacons of the station in her rear-view mirror, but they dwindled as she drove onward.

She turned the snowmobile right. She had glanced at the GPS coordinates earlier before speeding after Ted and the troop, making a mental note of where she had seen the meteors. She planned to orientate herself from there. The meteors had been off to the right, in the direction of the distant mountains, be-lieved to be the crater walls of Wilkes' Land mass concentration.

But the landscape was unrecognizable in the bliz-zard. She couldn't even see half a meter in front of her, much less any distant mountains. She slowed the snowmobile down to walking speed, 5 kmh. Some-how the wind was gusting in through her gloves and her fingers were starting to numb. The journey that had taken her thirteen minutes earlier in the day was going to take her longer at night. A lot longer. She glanced at her navigation, the green numbers glowed back at her reassuringly. This was an idiotic idea, she thought. I should turn back. Those meteors, if that's even what they were, have probably been buried by now.

But she had come this far. She knew she would be reprimanded when she returned, perhaps even deprived of any further reconnaissance time and expelled from the mission. If she retreated without the meteors the trip would be wasted. Check and see, check and see, the scientific theory reassured her. Materials are necessary for experiments.

She never saw what she hit. It might have been a snowdrift or even a half-buried meteor. One second she was sitting on the snowmobile, motoring through the Antarctican night, the next she was flying, thrown free from the driver's seat. Up became down and she tumbled through the air, hitting the snow with a muffled thud, the sound of which was stolen by the howling wind.

She awoke some time later, not sure of where she was or why there was snow in her mouth. She sat up with a start but her body didn't follow suit. Pain shot up her leg and she couldn't feel her fingers or toes.

The blizzard had stopped. The night was clear, the starlight sharp.

"Outpost 70, Outpost 70, Wilkes Base Station, are you there? Can anyone hear me? Hello?" she shouted into her microphone but there was no answer, not even a cackle of static.

She bit down the panic. She would just have to save herself. And, as much as she believed in the scientific theory, it wasn't going to rescue her.

She looked around and could make out the hulking shadow of her fallen snowmobile. She crawled forward, dragging her useless leg behind her.

The headlight was off and all the instruments were sideways. The navigation unit had gone dark. She located the compass but the needle was twirling across the glowing white letters representing the directions. Ted had warned them in the beginning that this sometimes happened, that they were to rely more on the GPS because sometimes the compasses went insane.

Every direction was north.

Cleo rolled onto her back to look at the sky. The stars were unfamiliar and ice clear, their light spiking into her brain. Had she somehow been transported to another planet? Another universe where she was the only living being? The place where Recce's Comet originated? The stars jittered and seemed to be rushing towards her. Her own heartbeat was thudded in her ears.

I'm at the end of the world, she panicked. I'm going to fall off. I'm going to be sucked right through the ozone hole into outer space where I'm going to go into orbit, then caught again by earth's gravity and I'm going to burn up, screaming across the sky like a meteorite.

She closed her eyes again and remembered back in her backyard in California, after she had been adopted, where she had seen her first meteor. But there had been a life before she had been adopted. The childhood behind the childhood.

She smacked the side of her helmet with her gloved hand. Her thoughts were like electrons in an atomic scattergun. She only felt her palm, her fingers had disappeared. Get a grip! You aren't in another uni-verse. You aren't going to burn up like a meteor. You aren't going to fall off the earth. You aren't going to die out here. You are going to right this snowmo-bile and motor back to the station and get your leg checked by Medical.

She rolled over and shoved her palms under the handlebars. She still couldn't feel her fingers. She pushed at the massive vehicle, bracing herself with her good leg. A spasm of agony ripped through the other leg anyway and she screamed but didn't stop pushing. Her good leg slipped in the snow. She con-centrated her energy and pushed again. She knew a snowmobile weighted about 450 lbs. but she tried to forget that as she shoved the snowmobile upward, working against gravity.

The snowmobile miraculously toppled upright in a rush and she collapsed across the seat, panting. She hauled her uncooperative body onto the vehicle and tried to start it. Fortunately the pedals were on the right side, the side of the leg that still worked.

The snowmobile only gurgled.

"Damn you! Damn you! Start!" Cleo slapped the gas tank with her palm. What was the freezing point of gasoline, she wondered.

-40°C

Oh yes, there was a reason why garages in Antarc-tica were heated. Yes indeedy.

There was something on the horizon. Dancing lights. She thought about ghost lights of Marfa, Texas.

Maybe she was about to discover the source? Or had the stars fallen to earth?

The lights were getting closer.

Then she heard the whine of snowmobiles.

A hot tear streaked down her frozen cheek. She was going to be rescued. She wasn't going to die out here in the cold.

It was Ted. He leapt from the snowmobile. He was shouting something but Cleo tapped the side of her helmet. The receiver had been damaged in the accident. He put his head so close to hers that their helmets clicked together. "You could have died out here! What are you crazy?" He grabbed her by her jacket and for a second Cleo thought he was going to shake her back and forth like an angry parent.

No, Cleo thought, but almost. She had almost died trying to find the beginning of life. The irony was not lost on Cleo, but she knew that Ted would never understand. She began weeping, Ted released his grip and she crumpled down into the snow like a broken doll.

"Don't go over there," Ted had said. And that ultra-masculine imperious brute had been right.

*

A man was rushing towards her. She could see him clearly. It wasn't night. She wasn't in Antarctica. She was in Switzerland. It wasn't Ted. It was the man from the hotel. That imaginary hat bastard!

She smirked, leaving the horrors of Antarctica behind her for the moment. "So, you stole my taxi and my porter, did you steal my meteorite as well?" She said as soon as he got within earshot. She halted and put her hands on her hips.

"Excuse me?" He halted, keeping his glove pressed against his nose.

"You're the man from the hotel."

"Yes I saw you there. With that frumpy lady and miserable young man." He moved his glove away and Cleona saw that his jacket had flecks of blood.

"Are you all right? Are you bleeding?"

"What? Oh." He rubbed his jacket briskly. "No it's nothing. I got a nosebleed, but it's stopped now. We saw much worse back in Vietnam, young lady. Much worse."

"Well, I have a doctorate but it's in geology, not medicine." She folded her arms. "It's probably a karma issue from when you stole my taxi. You better not have pilfered by meteorite as well."

"I don't have time for your frivolous diagnosis and empty threats," he barked and passed her roughly. "I don't have time for anything at all." He hurried away.

"What makes you think my threat is empty?" she called to his retreating back. She paused to watch him go, taking the opportunity to catch her breath. He scuttled away like the rabbit in Alice in Wonderland. What had he been up to out here? There were no other hikers around. Had he been to visit Lucia Zurbriggen? Was he interested in the meteorite as well? She rushed to follow his tracks upward.

She rounded a bend and then she saw it, the little cabin where the photograph had been taken. The same doorway. And Lucia Zurbriggen was still standing in it. With her dog. Cleona started waving.

"Ms. Zurbriggen? Ms. Zurbriggen!"

Lucia looked at her with the blank stare of the old who have forgotten their own birthday. Cleona mentally rubbed her hands together. This would be as easy as reciting the periodic table backwards, which Cleona did every night before she fell asleep.

"Haben Sie ihn gesehen?" Lucia called out.

"Pardon?" Cleo hurried forward.

"Dis man. He visit me."

"Yes ma'am. He passed me on my way up. He was headed back to town. Was he interested in your meteorite?"

"Do I know you?" The old woman looked completely bewildered, and Cleona smelling her chance, leaned in for the kill.

"No ma'am," she panted as she drew to a halt in front of her. "I'm from the International Science Committee, and I'm here to retrieve your meteorite, ma'am."

"My meteorite?"

"Yes, ma'am. The one you found a couple weeks ago."

Lucia shook her head slowly. "I cannot give you."

"Ma'am you have to. It belongs to the government."

"It fell out of sky, and I think sky belongs to no one."

"Yes but it fell on government property. All this land is a national park under government regulation." Her sweeping arm encompassed the entire mountain area. The performance was Oscar-worthy, the second time that day.

"No, science lady. This land is mine. From my family. A long time! I found rock, mountain teach me—finders-keepers. Rock is on my land now. You leave now. The same way like you come." She pointed down the mountain.

Cleona suddenly imagined herself pushing the old woman down—she would collapse like a house of cards under a good enough shove— marching into the cabin, overturning chairs, emptying out drawers and seizing the meteor from whatever place Ms. Zurbriggen might have hidden it. She glanced around. They were alone. She was sure she would be able to find the meteor. It would pull her like a nail to a magnet. She could already feel its tug from here.

She peered around Lucia, her eyes drawn to an exquisite box on Lucia's window sill. It was the right size to store a meteorite.

But she wasn't quite at that desperation level yet. Not yet. Besides, she didn't know if the dog would defend his mistress.

"Five thousand! I can offer you five thousand American dollars for it."

Lucia shook her head. "Not for sale. Not to buy, this rock."

The dog next to Lucia started growling and Cleo took a step back. "I'll just have to come back with the police. It would save you a lot of anguish and me a lot of time if you just hand it over now."

"Get out!" the old woman shouted.

Cleo took another step back, startled by the old lady's outburst. The dog stepped forward, his growl getting louder.

"This isn't over!" Cleona shook her finger at Lucia. "Do you hear me? I'll be back!" She marched back down the mountain.

Chapter 7

Cleona barged into her hotel room aflame with righteous anger that instantly converted to terror as a stranger charged towards her. Had she surprised a burglar? Had she locked the door? Or had it been open? Cleona froze and the person stopped directly in front of her. She flipped on the light. She was being robbed by her own reflection in the hotel mirror.

She rubbed her thin chest in an attempt to calm her thumping heart. The maid had drawn the drapes to keep out the stark afternoon sun and in the shadows she had mistaken her own reflected image for a burglar. My alter ego, she thought and she hiccupped a laugh, which sounded like the onset of madness in the empty room. Maybe I could engage her to get the meteor for me?

The shakes hit as the adrenaline ebbed from her bloodstream. She had surprised herself with the inability to persuade the meteor out of Lucia Zurbriggen, and the level of frustration at the botched collection attempt added to the tremors. It reminded her of the Antarctican folly, and Cleo did not take well to failure. As usual, she had forgotten to factor in the human element, the idea that Lucia Zurbriggen had become attached to the meteor. It was a mistake Cleo made repeatedly—she knew that when iron, oxygen and water combine, the iron loses electrons to the oxygen atoms—ten times out of ten trials. People were the unknown factor, their emotions were unpredictable. She had no inkling how an elderly lady could treasure a rock that she could use for any other purpose than a paperweight. I could have handled that better though, Cleo chided herself. I didn't have to shout at that old woman. She'll never give me the meteor now. I even threatened her! Because of the snow, she reasoned. She massaged her heart in hectic circles without realizing it. The Scientific Method didn't help me. The snow made me nervous. But snow wasn't what sabotaged me. I did that to myself.

She peeled off her puffy winter clothes with trembling fingers, not bothering to pick them off the bed to hang up. Her dark blue jacket was damp with melted snow and sweat, probably soaking through the bed sheets, but Cleona didn't care. I don't deserve nice things, she thought, I didn't earn my keep today. Her bathing suit lay at the bottom of the suitcase, she hadn't planned on needing it.

Ironically it had been the first thing she had packed. "Ow!"

One of the bathing suit straps had caught on the last remaining joint of her middle toe on the left foot—a mistake that only happened when she was not paying attention. She gingerly removed the strap from the deformed toe and slid the rest of it on. She worked her feet into flip flops, mindful of her missing toes. She slipped into a bathrobe, tucked a towel under her arm and marched off in search of the hotel swimming pool, leaving her villainous reflection behind.

The pool enclosure was done in Roman style with random pillars throughout the structure which held up nothing. The murals on the wall showed scenes of Roman temples, painted in light blue, green, white and gold. Multicolored lights lit the water from underneath and the Andermatts had even managed to make the chlorine smell more like a spring breeze than a disinfectant. Maybe they knew something about chemistry?

She flopped down in a lounge chair and squeezed her eyes shut to close out her massive defeat.

"Well, someone looks pissed."

Cleo opened her eyes and was surprised to find Zach towering above her. She noticed that he had a couple starter hairs peeking through the opening of his white terrycloth bathrobe.

"Are you talking to me?" It was an unlikely probability, but Cleo had to ask.

"No, I'm talking to the invisible guy lying on top of you."

"Well, your sarcasm hasn't changed and your humor hasn't improved, so it must be you, Zach, the perpetually angry teenager." Cleo sat up. She instinctively didn't like to be lying down when he was standing so close to her.

"Well, excuse the fuck out of me. I saw you lying there looking like you were about to explode so I wanted to see if you needed an ambulance or a psychiatrist or something." He was grinning, taking some sort of strange pleasure in her distress.

"What I need is to be left alone." She squeezed her eyes closed again.

She heard the lounge chair next to hers groan as he sat down on it.

"I didn't ask you to sit down," she said without opening her eyes.

"Well, it's a free country. At least I think it is."

"Switzerland is a direct democracy. So technically it is a free country."

"Oh yeah? Then why does everything cost so fucking much?"

Cleona opened her eyes and saw him grinning at her. "Was that your idea of a joke?"

He nodded. "C'mon. Spill. I'll go away if you tell me why you are so mad."

"Why do you care?"

He shrugged. "I don't really. But I don't have anything else to do or anyone else to annoy at the moment."

She sighed. "Well, remember the meteorite I was talking about last night? The reason I came all the way to Switzerland?"

"Oh yeah, I was hardly listening."

"Well, to give you the synopsis version, I attempted to go get it today and the old lady who found it won't give it to me. I think she would rather eat oxidized nails and drink boric acid than release it."

"Yeah, well, she wouldn't just want to give it to you. I guess a meteorite is a pretty special thing, but I don't know for sure because I take naps in Earth Science class. That might explain why I got the D."

"I even offered to buy it!" Cleona pounded the chair in frustration and caught her fist between the slats.

She had to yank it out, catching the tip of her missing finger and wincing.

"Really? For how much?"

"500," Cleona lied. She didn't want to admit that Ms. Zurbriggen had turned down 5000.

"Well, now. For 500 I could steal it for you."

Cleona opened her mouth to vehemently decline his offer but then snapped it closed again. How could she even contemplate it? He was a minor, and she knew, and even sort of liked, his mother, or at least felt sorry for her.

"You're trying to trick me," she accused. "If I say yes, you will run to your mother and tell her how I tried to corrupt you and steal your innocence."

"Hah! Do I look like a guy who goes running to his mommy? Do I look as though I have any innocence left? What I do need is money. How old is this lady?"

"Ancient, at least."

"Sounds like an easy job."

A thought occurred to Cleona. "You've been in trouble with the law, haven't you? Your Mom mentioned that. Was it for burglary?"

His eyes clouded. "I don't have to answer that. Let me just put it this way, old women and I don't seem to get along. Look, do you want me to do it or not?"

They regarded each other as Cleona considered the offer, his brown eyes held her gaze without flinching. Rather unusual for a man so young, almost admirable. Tiny waves lapped against the wall of the pool. She thought of all that snow. At night.

"I think she keeps it in a box on her window sill."

"I can get it for you," he said. "500. Deal?"

"Okay," she answered, and she felt her soul depart as if she had just sold it to the devil.

Neither one of them noticed the beached whale of Vera lounging in the shadows in the corner, counting her own fingers with amazing concentration.

The night was glass clear and Zachary felt as though he were being observed as he loped up the mountain. He hadn't counted on was how deep the snow was. Why hadn't that science bitch suggested he wear snowshoes? She might know a lot about geology, he thought as slush slid into his boots, but she didn't know crap about snow. His ankle socks were sopped. Not to mention he was wearing the wrong clothes for a robbery. His body heat was melting the snow on his jeans and they were soaked. His sweat felt slicky sick on his skin, like the way it felt during his last fever. He had been cold at first, but now he was starting to go numb. Not to mention that he stuck out around here like a rhinoceros. It was dark but he was plenty visible against the snow. More appropriate would have been a James Bond-like totally white snowsuit. Fortunately there was no one out here to notice or not notice him. It was like being on another planet, marching through the night-blued snow. The drifts glowed with an otherworldly light.

There were no trail markings or handrails. His thin gloves were already wet with chunks of ice clinging to them. Cleo had told him straight up the mountain, it's the only cabin up there, you can't miss it. The amount of snow on the boulders increased as he ascended. They were no longer recognizable as rocks, only giant snow balls. As he trudged over the first incline and there was no little cabin in sight, he realized he might get lost. The slushy orange streetlight-lit roads of the village seemed like a dream away. Why hadn't he thought to ask Cleona how far away it was? Any paths there might have been were buried under the thick blanket of snow. They would only be revealed in spring thaw—like his dead body would be.

He rounded a bend and let out a pent-up breath, escaping smoke-like into the night air. There it was—a house-shaped shadow crouching in a snow drift. Relief emboldened his stride as he approached the little cabin. It looked as dark as his Math teacher's heart but if he was lucky it would be warm. Although he knew that he wasn't going inside for a cup of hot cocoa and to put his feet up by the fire, at least a burglary offered a respite from freezing his ass off in Mother Fucking Nature.

Zach had been in a lot of places in his life where he shouldn't have been. He knew how to sneak into the girls' locker room at school. He had figured out how to get into the air duct above the ladies bathroom. When his father had grounded him and locked his bedroom door he shimmied down the drain pipe from the second floor into freedom.

But he had never broken into anyone's house before.

He stopped at what he judged to be a safe-from-being-seen distance from the little cabin. He fingered his young beard hairs, trying to decide to approach from the front or the side or the back. The thick snow made it impossible to 'case' the house. He was aware of the deep footprints he was leaving behind, and it wasn't snowing so they would not be covered. Could police take casts from snow? The science lady hadn't told him that, either.

He looked behind him. He could still turn back, follow his own footprints. But he had come this far and he was freezing his balls off and he could buy a lot of Nintendo games for five hundred dollars.

Might as well get it over with. The best way was just to go in the front door. He was half-surprised to find it unlocked.

The moon and the light reflected from the snow lit up the little room in a ghostly glow. He froze when he saw the dog in the corner. It was a golden retriever, a big one. The dog woke up, looked at him, and then lay back down, uninterested. Zachary breathed out in measures. Why hadn't she mentioned the dog? He was going to extort more money out of her when he got back for sure. The trip alone had been twice as difficult as he had imagined. Now, let's find that rock and get out of here, he coached himself.

A gold-colored box by the window caught his eye, shining in the moonlight. At least she had told him about that. He gently lifted the lid. It was like a small cradle inside, lined with blue velvet. Weird, he thought. Like a coffin for a baby. The meteorite inside was nothing remarkable, seemingly unworthy of such a luxurious bed. It looked like an ordinary rock to Zachary. As he closed the box he heard an answering click behind him. He turned around and was looking right into two pitch-black holes of a gun barrel.

"Lass das sein!"

"What?"

"Drop it, mister man. You don't take the old lady's treasure."

Zachary obeyed. He was terrified. He had never looked down the barrel of a gun before. And he did really have to look down because the old woman holding the gun was shorter than he was. He realized this in the millisecond it took for the box to hit his foot.

The pain was sharp and immediate. "Ah fuck!" Zach shouted and started hopping up and down on his uninjured foot.

"Bad language," Lucia frowned. "My dog don't like bad language." She sighed and put the rifle down. "You are no good at robbing. You all right? You hurt?"

"It would probably be worse if I had all the feeling back in my feet, but I think I caught frostbite on the goddamn way up here."

"Pah!" She let go of the gun with one hand and pinched his jacket between two bony fingers. "Too thin for mountains. Where you come from?"

"I walked all the way from Zermatt village."

„In winter! At night! You want my rock very much." She put the rifle aside, picked up the box and sat down at her table. She pushed the folding chair out for him with her foot. "Tell me now why."

He crossed his arms. "What makes you think I'm going to tell you?"

"You broke into my house. This not legal."

"It wasn't locked. I was only looking for a place to get in out of the cold."

"No one is hiking at three in the morning! Only crazy people!" She wound a crooked finger around her ear.

"I had a fight with my mother."

Lucia winked at him. "You have a lot of answers, but I no believe not even one. You came for rock. Tell me why."

Zach crossed his arms. "I think I need a lawyer."

"You don't need lawyer, young man. Honest men no need lawyers. Make you a deal." She leaned forward. "You sit down. You tell me why. I get you dry socks. I make you chocolate. I no tell police. If not," she patted the rifle. "You go back into cold with empty hands and wet socks!"

Zachary didn't take long to consider his options. He hadn't had much luck lately with senior citizens. This one seemed spunky and nimble, completely capable and competent on her own turf. And she had a gun. And a dog. Their gazes were locked and hers didn't waver. Karma was finally catching up with him. "Okay."

She grunted and motioned to the chair. Zach sunk into it gratefully. Lucia smiled and Zach noted that she had no teeth left. No wonder her voice sounded so mushy. Lucia realized it at the same time. "Ooops, forgot my choppers." She took the rifle with her into her bedroom at the back of the little cabin and came back with a pair of wool socks and her dentures in but, Zach noted, without the gun. She put some milk over the fire in the fireplace and then ran her fingers over her dog's stomach. „Not even one bark, Spark." The dog sighed and let out a long fart. „Not good watch dog. But dog knows people," she sized up Zach, "He think you are okay. Would you have hurt me—an old woman?" She sat down again.

"You don't know me at all, lady. And you can be glad you don't. I'm not really good with old women. Not at all."

"So you don't come to visit old lady if you no like old ladies. What a nice boy want an ugly rock for?"

"It's not for me, I could give a shit about rocks." Lucia frowned at his word choice but said nothing. "It's for a lady scientist I met at the hotel—Cleona Skye. She said she would pay me if I stole the rock from you for her."

"How much she pay you?"

"She said she would give me five hundred dollars."

The milk started to softly bubble over the fire and Lucia got up to add the chocolate powder and give it a stir. "It's milk straight from the cow. What's your name?"

"Zach."

"Well, Zach. This Cleona Syke. She visit me earlier."

"I know. She told me."

"She said she pay me five thousand." She poured the cocoa into two mugs with a steady hand. She smiled at Zach. She put a cup in front of him and pushed his mouth shut with her palm. „Close your mouth, young man. Flies sleep all winter, no flies here."

"She left that part out."

"And you—what? Make crime and maybe my dog eat you—"She gave the sleeping dog a pat on the head. "Frostbite! For only five hundred. This not fair."

"No it isn't."

Lucia nodded and said, "You must be all right. Sparky, he no eat you. He only eat evil. But he also no eat Cleona Syke or this Reginald … "

"Who?"

"An old American soldier. He forgot his treasure." She pulled the crystal out of her pocket. "It's like train station on a Saturday here, so many visit! But only you get cocoa."

"Lucky me then." Zach took a sip and almost choked. „What the f—fudge?"

Lucia barked a laugh. "Little rum to warm belly, no worries."

"It's good." Zach took another sip.

"Maybe she not evil, Cleona Skye, but she do not nice things. We teach her a lesson."

Zach wiped milk foam off with the back of his hand. "I'm not interested in getting back at anyone. I think it's probably better if I go back and tell her I couldn't do it. And she can keep her five hundred dollars. We can just forget this ever happened."

"You help me now. You want to rob my house! You could have died on mountain, very dangerous at night! Wolves! Meteroites! For five hundred dollars? Pah! What if you lost the way?"

Zachary flushed. The skin of his cheeks began to prickle pink as the feeling returned. His feet started to warm up turning his socks into little saunas. He eyed the dry socks greedily. "What did you have in mind?"

She pushed the socks across the table to him and winked. Her smooth face wrinkled up for a moment in a bud of pure happiness. She heaved herself up and her dog watched her with one open eye. Zach heard her rummaging about in the back room, clicks, bangs and tinkles, sounding like she was digging deep into a drawer. She came back with a green plastic bowl and a shoebox with a white bottle balanced on top. She opened the box and proudly presented Zachary with tiny glass bottles, some filled with sand and some with pebbles. "My cousin she go to Italy on holiday once. I ask her bring me back some beach. I never see ocean, you know. My ocean only snow and sky. Nothing forever, mind you. Nothing can be put in a bottle or held in hand or treasured. Bottled snow turns to water. Last week part of sky fell. A part can hold in my hands. Since then, I have much visitors. Much interest in piece of heaven."

She ran her finger dreamily along the glass bottle. "We make rock for Dr. Skye." She lifted the box back on the table and lifted out the meteorite. "Must look like this."

She shook a layer of sand into the bowl and doused it with white liquid from the brown bottle—glue. Then she added a layer of pebbles and handed Zachary the glue. "Here. You do some too."

"You want to make a fake meteorite?" Zach raised one of his eyebrows, shifting his gaze from the meteorite to the growing mess in the bowl. "But the color is wrong. Can you get me some cocoa powder?"

She brought it and he dumped in half a can until the mixture darkened. He tried to stir the glop with the wooden spoon she handed him but the batter was so thick he gave up, the spoon jaunting out at a jolly angle. He wiggled it back out. "It's still not dark enough. Do you have anything else?"

She handed him another bottle. "Polish for shoes."

He shook out half the container. "How can we stir this? Do you have any gloves?"

She zipped back into the kitchen and returned with the ugliest oven mitts he had ever seen, looking as though they might have been new in the seventies, decorated with gaudy hot pink and orange flowers. He shrugged as he slipped them on. "They will have to do."

In the center of the concoction she planted the crystal Reginald had left behind. "This make it look real," she declared.

Zach shrugged again. This lady had great powers of imagination.

"Ok, put in lots of glue now," she directed. He did as she wished and kneaded the mixture like dough with the oven mitts.

"And for the finishing touch!" Zach shed the clumpy mitts, dug out a crumpled gum wrapper from his wet pocket and pushed it into the mess with his thumb.

Lucia beamed her approval and swung the bowl

from the table, almost knocking over the cocoa. "Perfect! Now outside to dry."

"Is drying the same as freezing?"

"No matter, will get hard." She pushed her window open and put the bowl outside. The sudden blast of cold air made Zach shiver in his wet jeans.

"How long will it take?"

"Never made a rock before, but is very cold so not long." She closed the window, sat back down and surveyed him. "You will freeze on the way back. I never married, can no give you husband's clothes. But give me your pants to dry by fire. And now you change socks."

"That would be very kind of you ma'am."

She smiled. "I am Lucia, no ma'am."

"I'm Zachary. Thank you, Lucia."

"Zachariah is good bible name." She nodded.

Zachary wiggled out of his pants—why do they get tighter when wet?—and handed them sheepishly over. Lucia draped them by the fire without ceremony, as if having a half-naked teenager in her home was the new norm. He sat down again.

"You tell me now Zachary why you need money?" She straightened his jeans over a bar. "Your family here on vacation, cost a lot!"

Zachary blushed again in the firelight. "My family is not exactly well-off. It's only my mom and me."

"Your father?"

"He remarried and lives in another state."

"Your mother have money?"

"She saved a long time for this vacation. She wanted to take me here."

"She really love you, then."

"I'm sure she does, but we don't get along so well."

"Why not?"

He hung his head. "I'm going through some stuff that she can't understand."

"What she no understand?"

"I did something really bad, Lucia. And I guess she doesn't know how to deal with it."

"Maybe she should yell at you more."

"Maybe."

"If you were mine you would shovel snow! All winter!" She cackled.

They watched the fire in companionable silence sipping rum and cocoa as they waited for the fake rock and Zachary's pants to dry. It was cozy in the little cabin and Zach must have dozed off because the next thing he knew Lucia's bony finger was burrowing into his shoulder.

"Wake up Zachariah! Look what we make!"

Zach coaxed his eyes open, feeling embarrassed at falling asleep. But Lucia didn't care, her eyes were glowing, her whole face shone like a much younger woman's as she presented the 'meteorite' to him.

"Voilà!"

Zach choked back a laugh. No miracle had happened in the frozen night. The mass they had produced looked exactly like what it was ... .pebbles, shells, glue and a hodge-podge of junk from the depths of Lucia's cabinets. He even spotted gaudy strands of oven mitt. "That looks terrible! And look, half of this disaster is curved the same shape as the bowl! She'll never believe this is a meteorite, not for one second!"

"Ah, but the weight—" She handed him the fake rock to hold. He hefted it dutifully. Then she took it back and passed him the real meteorite.

He shrugged. "Yes, ok, they weigh about the same. But she's gonna know—"

"Of course! She is real scientist! Here, you do this—" she handed him a knife and pointed to the fake meteor. "Take some pieces off round part, make it look realer." Zach attacked the jumble like a sculptor on steroids but it was tough going. The fake rock was more solid than a real one, the glue had hardened into concrete in the sub subzero air. He had to chuckle as he chiseled. Here he was, in some strange old woman's cabin at the end of the world in his underwear, chipping chucks off some insane art project. Anson would be cracking up if he could see him. Life was full of weirdness.

"There!" He showed off his labor proudly. The project looked less rounded, more weathered and random. With enough imagination, it could have been flying through space.

Lucia grinned like an eight-year-old girl and brushed away some dust. She opened the box and put the false meteor inside. "Now here is the trick." She took a little golden padlock from her apron pocket and locked the box. "Won't keep her out for long ... .but maybe long enough for you to get paid. You a smart boy, you figure it out." She folded her arms and nodded her satisfaction.

"I'm sure I will," Zach answered. "But I need my pants back first, please, Lucia."

"Of course." She tossed the crispy jeans to Zach. "And to keep dry, you use my shoe shoes. You will walk on snow like Jesus on water!" She cackled and handed him the snowshoes.

Chapter 8

The sand kept escaping through cracks in the wooden floor as she attempted to sweep it up. Lucia, being unfamiliar with the beach, didn't know about the tendency of individual grains of sand to evade capture. The sand glimmered stubbornly in the morning sunlight, remnants of her art project the night before. It was rough under her bare feet and clung to her skin, even Sparky was tip-toeing around the strange stuff. She had never taken it out before, she had planned on keeping it bottled up forever. But she wasn't sorry, it had been great fun.

"Memories aren't supposed to be bottled up," she told Sparky. "They are meant to be taken out and used as building materials for new experiences." She only wished that she could hold on to her own memories. She was trying to coax stubborn grit into the dustpan when there was a knock at the door.

Lucia looked over at Sparky. "Someone's come to visit," she told him. "Something new." She laughed. Her back cracked as she straightened up, and she had to lean on the broom for a second before opening the door.

Lately Sparky had been paying visitors no attention but this one made him raise his shaggy head. A beautiful blonde angel stood in the doorway, white flowing robes waving around her body. She had on hot pink padded boots which had the label 'Moon

Boots' running vertically up her leg. Behind her was an army of geriatrics, also draped in white. Their ancient and blank faces were the only things that differentiated them from the snow.

"I am Astra, high priestess of the Children of the Snowflake. Fear not, mortal woman. I have come to relieve you of the burden of God's soul."

"What, Missy? You want to kill me?" Sparky lunged to his feet, as if understanding the word "kill".

"In no way, madam, would I harm any of God's creatures. I am their protectress." The sun shone behind her giving her an otherworldly aura. "I mean the message sent from God. That you found. I am here to receive it."

"Message from God?"

"Yes, the falling star. God sent me to retrieve it. I am the only one who can decode its message."

"I tell everyone already a hundred times! It's my meteorite, I keep it!"

"Really, madam, I must insist. We have travelled far—"Her posse behind her bobbed their heads in unison "—to claim what we feel is our birthright."

"If meteorite yours you would have found it."

"It was God's will that we search for it."

"God like treasure hunt? Look, lady, you and your friends go quest something else. The meteorite, she is mine. I tell you nice goodbye. Next I get my gun and send my dog ... " Sparky marched to Lucia's side.

Astra looked at the dog and considered. "All right, we will go. I can see that there is no reasoning with you now. We will go set up camp just outside your property so that we will be close by when you change your mind. We'll be over there." Astra pointed to just behind a half-buried fence.

"You don't stay here," Lucia said. "Cold as a witch's tit at night. You kill all these old and crazy people if you stay here."

"Our faith keeps us warm. These people are my lambs, they will follow me to the end of the earth if I request it, or at least as far as they can walk. It's actually your fault and your responsibility if we suffer any losses while we wait in the cold. We made it all the way over here, and we have no intention of leaving until we get what we want."

"This never happen," Lucia promised.

"It will. God sent me a vision, and he promised me. You can't keep us out forever. You have to sleep sometime." There was nothing angelic about her smile as she turned and directed her followers to set up camp.

Cleona was dreaming that she was being chased through the night sky by an Abominable Snowman/Yeti type monster. He was pelting stars at her like snowballs. She took up refuge behind the Big Dipper to the dismay of the Yeti. He started punching the constellation with his fist. She peered over the spoon handle into his stupid, icy blue eyes but the knocking didn't stop.

She was ripped out of her dream into her hotel room, already flooded by golden sunlight. She dreamed more in the mountains, and those dreams were vivid. But the knock was real. She leapt out of bed and whipped open the door.

"Hmmm," Zach said. He turned his head away. "Couldn't you at least put some clothes on?"

Cleo looked down and saw she had fallen asleep in her bra and boxers. "Never mind that! Come in, come in." She yanked him inside. "Did you get it?"

Zach nodded and held out the box he had been carrying. Cleo snatched for it but he hugged it back to his chest and shook his head. "First the money, we had a deal."

Cleo winked. "You are a natural born criminal. Your mother should maybe try to develop your talent instead of squash it."

"You don't have to kiss my ass anymore. I did what you wanted me to. All I want now is my money and I'll leave you and your rock alone to get acquainted. Besides, I didn't get into trouble for robbery. My crime was more serious."

"Assault, then, maybe? For someone who didn't pay you?"

"You don't need to know. Let's just say I don't like to be kept waiting."

Cleo rolled her eyes at his dramatics but strode to the hotel safe in the closet and retrieved an envelope. She counted the money out on the table in front of him. "Three hundred, four hundred, five hundred." They exchanged treasures. Cleona took the box gingerly from him and placed it on her desk. "Hey, it's locked!"

He flipped the lock with his finger. "It's only a suitcase lock. You can probably break it with a kitchen knife."

"Do you think you could—?"

Zach shook his head. "Look lady we're even. Like I said, I wasn't arrested for robbery. The rest you have to do yourself. I'll leave and let you get started."

But to Cleo it was as if he no longer existed. All her attention was focused on the golden box. Zachary slipped out, gently pulling the room door closed instead of slamming it. Wait until she found out! But she might not be so wrong about him after all, he thought as he sauntered down the hall to his room.

He had memorized her combination when she had opened the safe.

Zach slunk through the hallways, imagining himself to be an American Secret Agent. He returned to his room and lay down on the bed, playing with the hundred dollar bills when his mother barged into the room. He had been holding the bills flat in his hand and swiping them on the bedspread, a trick he had seen on Youtube. As soon as she entered he snatched them back up and shoved them under his pillow.

"Where have you been," she demanded. I was looking for you."

"I took a walk." Zach leaned back on the pillow.

Since when do teenage boys take walks, Amanda thought, but she let it slide. "I wanted to go to breakfast. I'm pretty hungry after skiing yesterday. I think the mountain air increases my appetite. And you?"

He shrugged.

"Well, do you want to come down to the restaurant with me?"

"Not really."

Amanda kneaded her hands and her left eye ticked. "Honey, I have to ask you something and it's really hard for me."

"Better not ask then."

"I have to. It's my job. Being your parent is really not easy." She sighed and pressed her fists together. "Where were you last night?"

The air in the hotel room, the mountain air that encouraged such hunger, all of a sudden became charged with eddies of distrust and undercurrents of resentment.

"What do you mean?" Zach measured her with slanted, dead eyes.

"I heard you get up. I'm not deaf, you know? We're sleeping in the same room and today there's a huge pile of wet clothes in the bathroom. Zach, are you taking drugs?"

"No."

"Well, where were you then last night?"

"I went for a beer. In Switzerland I am legal drinking age, I told you."

"Where?"

"In town."

"Zachary, your clothes from last night are soaked! Not only that, you couldn't be bothered to hang them up. Now tell me, really, where were you last night?"

"I got drunk and fell in a snowbank."

She shook her head. "I don't believe that."

"You don't believe anything I say. That's your problem."

"You're right about that, it is my problem! You're

only 16 which makes you a minor, legal drinking age or not, so I'm responsible for you. And you're on probation. If something happens while we're over here it's my butt on the line too!"

"It's always about you, isn't it? What a poor thing you are having a kid like me! Well, I didn't get a bargain either, you couldn't even keep Dad! How do you think you're going to keep me?"

He leapt up and grabbed his jacket, the one that was dry.

"Where are you going?" she pleaded as he shoved his feet in his shoes.

"Out!" And he slammed the door behind him.

Amanda stood frozen in the middle of the room. She literally did not know what to do next. Then the paralysis broke and she hurried over to the bed and checked under the pillow. She had seen that he had hidden something here when she had come into the room and she was right. She pulled out the crumpled bills and burst into tears.

Cleona adjusted the desk lamp over the box. She had spread a white plastic cloth under it and set up a camera to record history. She knew she should wait until she was back in the lab, but she couldn't. Only Darwin and Nelson Mandela had that amount of patience. She wouldn't be able to do a full analysis of the meteor in her hotel room, but a preliminary investigation was possible. And just to hold it in her hands! She opened her silver suitcase and removed a miniature test tube holder and a tiny chisel and hammer. She turned the camera on and then snapped on her plastic gloves, so tight they nearly cut off circulation at her wrists. The rubber tube where her missing digit was supposed to occupy drooped despondently down.

"Date is February 21, time 9:38 am. I am just about to begin the—" The what, actually? The inquiry? The inquisition? The dissection, for God's sake? "—the investigation." She winked at the camera before she started on the lock. She was half afraid that history would see her incompetence at picking locks but Zach was right, it opened on the first tug from her hook. She lifted the lid and frowned. The meteor looked different than the picture she had clipped from the journal. "Visual examination reveals a gritty substance as the base, almost like sand. There is no way this could have survived a fall through earth's atmosphere."

"The color is not homogenous." She rubbed it with her gloved fingers. "Odd. It crumbles with touch. Extremely fragile. What is this—?" She broke off as she noticed a silver glint.

"There seems to be some sort of metal vein here, thin like foil, I wonder if it's iron. I'm going to get a sample." She wiggled it loose with a pair of tweezers. "Huh?" She smoothed the material out on the desk.

Wrigley's.

She yanked the photograph out of her back pocket. The dog. The old woman. The meteorite. The rock Lucia was holding in the picture looked nothing like the compressed garbage pile in front of her.

"I'm going to kill that kid." She told the camera.

Cleona found him again by the pool, no bathrobe this time, he was fully dressed in a jacket and boots.

"Well, that didn't take long," he said as she stormed over, not bothering with flip-flops.

"My primary analysis has determined that the early universe is composed of Elmer's glue and Juicy Fruit. Ha ha, very funny, you asshole. Now give me my money back."

"No can do, lady."

"You better can do! What the hell were you thinking?"

"It was that old lady's idea, the one you wanted me to rob. Lucia. She caught me in her house and she said that she would report me to the police if I didn't go along with her. It was kind of fun." He leaned back and laced his hands behind his head. "And I actually can't think of anyone who deserves to be tricked more than you. Look at it this way—you only lost 500. I heard that you offered Lucia 10 times that amount."

"I can't afford to lose even 50. I'm on stipendium!"

He shrugged. "Not my problem. You should have thought of that before you contracted a burglary."

Cleona fumed. "It was all your idea! You were the one who offered to break into her house! And I don't care if you both sang Kumbaya while working on your arts and crafts project, I just want my money back. Now! Or I'll go to the police myself."

Zachary barked a laugh. "And tell them what? Your contracted burglary was botched? Forget it, science lady. I could have died out there. You got what you deserved."

"I'll tell your mother. That's what I'll do."

"My mother wouldn't do shit. She doesn't dare."

Cleona growled. That was true enough. She wrung her hands, she was out of threats.

He heaved himself out of the chair. "Look, in my opinion I think you should take it up with Ms. Zurbriggen if you're pissed. The fake meteor was her idea, and she's not exactly happy with you, either."

"Maybe I'll do just that." Cleo crossed her arms and tapped her foot.

"You do that, science lady. See you at dinner. Might be an interesting one tonight." Zach marched away.

Cleona stood by the empty swimming pool. The water was perfectly still and the lights made the surface look like stained glass from a church. It's only a setback, she thought to herself. All great scientists have setbacks. It makes the discovery even more satisfying. I have to keep believing, she thought. The meteorite is still there. Which means I can still acquire it. Think about the Scientific Method. Maybe I need to sing a little Kumbaya myself.

She made herself smile, forcing herself to hum as she strutted down the hallway back to her room. Cleona felt she had something hard in her, something like chewing the foil wrapper instead of the gum. She was more determined than ever to get the meteor.

Chapter 9

When she was certain that the flock was busy preparing soup for lunch, Astra snuck a little ways out of camp and stood on the edge of a cliff, taking in the scenery. The pristine mountains and crystal blue sky were lost on her—such a beautiful setting for Astra's foul mood. She kicked a snowbank with her furry boot, muttering a choice swear word as snow slid into her sock.

Time to face facts—this had been a mistake. That Lucia woman was tougher than Astra expected. Astra had kept the flock awake in shifts to just stare at the tiny cabin, but Lucia ignored them. Lucia and her goddamn dog. Astra wasn't as holy as her congregation thought she was, but she did like dogs. She liked all animals, actually, and didn't want to harm any of them. But the dog definitely complicated things. He would give warning if anyone tried to sneak in. He might even bite. Astra couldn't charm him with her looks or sweet talking. If anyone threatened Lucia, he might snap a chunk out of their leg, spit it out, and come back for a second helping.

And her flock giving her looks this morning. They were still hooded glances—when she caught someone staring at her they had the decency to look away—but she saw at the edge of her vision that the seeds of doubt had been planted. It was freezing cold, and she had taken her nursing home camping. The night had hit 10 below Celsius. Old toes and fingers got cold fast. The longer they remained out here, the more likely it was that she would lose the trust of her people. The fires of rebellion were made of ice.

As she walked back to camp, she noticed the dog, Sparky, sitting above the camp and watching her intently. She darted into the makeshift kitchen and grabbed one of the last pork sausages.

"Come here," she called. "Come here boy."

She saw that he was torn. He sensed that she was one of the bad guys but any human holding a sausage couldn't be too evil, could they?

Astra started pulling off pieces and threw them in his direction. He gave in to his stomach and came snuffling towards her. She walked backwards, luring him into her tent. She still held half a sausage in her hand. He sat down primly and offered her his paw. She smiled as she shook it. He was a good dog, an excellent dog. It would be a damn shame if something happened to him.

Lucia woke up from her nap to the sound of Sparky scratching at the door. She had been dreaming about when there had been wolves in the mountains, with teeth of ice and eyes of fire, so she was grateful to him for waking her. She opened the heavy iron latch and pushed open the door. Sparky was wearing something around his neck. "What have you found now, boy?" She bent down with some difficulty to examine him. It was a piece of paper on a wire. Someone had put a sign around Sparky's neck.

"Who do you love more, me or the meteorite?"

Lucia held the paper in her hands and her blood ran cold.

Reginald didn't need to make lists—roster lists, shopping lists, lists of his favorite movies. He remembered all his soldiers, everything he ever bought and every scene of every film he ever watched. But he kept lists anyway. His primary school history teacher had recommended that as a way to help order the chaos in his mind. Like his scrapbook served as storage, the lists were like file cabinets. The lists forced him to concentrate and focus on only one thing at a time. He took comfort in the act of writing things down and ranking them. He had no wife, no family, no pets, no hobbies to otherwise occupy him. He was retired, he had time.

On the morning after his nosebleed he was sitting at his hotel desk, making a list of strange and unusual ways to die. He hoped to distract himself from reliving the nosebleed, which had unnerved him, by thinking of ways to bite the bullet, perhaps insert a slice of black humor in the situation.

He remembered the odd deaths from a lifetime of television-watching, newspaper-reading and radio-listening. For example, there was a Canadian folk singer who had been killed by coyotes. An Athenian law maker was smothered to death as he was covered in cloaks meant to honor him. There was a man struck in the face and killed by an airborne fire hydrant. How it got airborne was not revealed.

Once a seagull dropped a tortoise on the head of a bald man, apparently mistaking him for a stone, and killed him. There was a man who died after winning a cockroach eating contest. In Belarus it was death by beaver when, while trying to pose with it, the beaver bit into a fisherman's leg and snagged his artery. The fisherman bled to death. Mike Ellis, who had played with a band called Electric Light Orchestra, was killed when a rolling bale of hay hit his truck.

All of these were more newsworthy than his ordinary brain tumor.

Reginald laid his pen aside and gazed out the window. The day was brilliant, the snow hurt his eyes. He knew that Death could come at him full face or it could surprise him by attacking him from the side like a velaciraptor or could even sneak up on him from behind. It could be a turtle or a fire hydrant or a bale of hay. Or it could be a cancer eating his brain. There were so many ways to die. And Death felt close now. The verdict had been decided and now he only had to kill time while he waited for the sentence to be carried out.

"I'm not ready yet," he told the empty room. Why aren't you ready? the empty room asked him in return. You have seen men younger than you die for something they could hardly understand, much less believe in. You have had a full life. And your time is approaching. You are old. Why aren't you ready to die?

He rubbed his forehead with his fingertips. His brain felt as full as 11 gallons of water in a 10 gallon jug. Maybe he had to download all his thoughts and experiences somewhere or he wouldn't be able to let this life go.

It is she who will find you, Private Miller had said.

"Have you ever loved someone?" Lucia had asked.

Reginald shook his head. The train of these thoughts was going off-track. He decided to list the top ten causes of death in human beings instead. Not unusual this time, just commonplace. At least war didn't make the list. Rank and file, rank and file. First he would rank them and then file them away. If he could name the enemy, dissect it, analyze it, it wouldn't be so menacing. He would become familiar with death. He put his coffee mug next to his tablet. He did his research on the Internet these days, glad he had taken the Computers for Seniors course.

The leading causes of death in senior citizens were (in descending order) heart disease, then cancer, chronic lower respiratory diseases, accidents, stroke Alzheimer's, diabetes, influenza and pneumonia, nephritis and suicide.

"Have you ever loved someone?" Lucia had asked.

Suicide: Taking one's own life. Could this be honorable in a samurai sort of way or was it the ultimate cowardice? Was that the only option left for him faced with the horrors of everything else? Maybe he should consider it. It would give him back control of when and how to die.

Reginald put his pencil down again. The distraction wasn't working at all. Instead of breaking death down, he had only succeeded in raising its black specter in his hotel room. He looked up and saw that it was still 11:07. The hotel clock had stopped working. That is to say that the two hands counting minutes and hours had frozen, and the thin hand counting the seconds kept ticking mindlessly in circles, counting the same minute over and over.

So many ways to die. Like being at a convergence of many paths. Some are steep and rocky, like the trail he took to Lucia's house, some are wide and flat like streets in smalltown Pennsylvania but they all lead to the same place. The blackness. The 'over'. The end of Mildred and Billy's boy Reginald C. Patterson. And that's where he was heading, whichever path he took.

He snatched the pencil and threw it across the room. "How can I be dying?" he complained to the wall. "I haven't even lived yet! I have never been a father or naked in a jacuzzi or driven a go-cart or done yoga and the one person I could have loved had the audacity to die and left me all alone!"

He jumped when the phone rang. He snatched it angrily off the receiver. "Hello? Hello?"

There was no answer, no one on the other end.

He remembered that the phone had rung at Dr. Nussbaum's office, but when Brandy had answered it, no one was there.

Suddenly he became convinced that something was looking for him, and that something was his own death.

"Come and get me then! If you want me so badly, you know where I am, come and get me!" He shouted into the telephone, then slammed it down.

Cleona got back to her room and sighed at the remnants of the fake meteor. What a mess! How could I have been so stupid to fall for that? She swiped the main piece of the fake meteorite into the black mesh garbage can and the sand broke apart, revealing all the strange components of the rock. Something solid glinted from the wreckage. Cleona's trained eye recognized it right away as crystal. She picked it up.

"Could it be—?"

She was interrupted by a knock at the door.

"Housekeeping!"

She slipped the crystal in her lab coat pocket and went to go open the door. At least the reminders of her stupidity would now be swept away by the hotel maid.

Anyway, it was time to pay Lucia Zurbriggen another visit.

Zach returned to the hotel room around lunchtime, after getting hungry and discovering that he had stormed out of his hotel room without his 500 dollars. He charged into the room and then stopped short.

The beds had been made.

"Oh fuck." He rushed over to his bed and ripped the pillow off. The money was gone.

He beat down the impulse to start tearing the room apart. The maid wouldn't have moved the money, she would have pocketed it.

He raced downstairs and found Emma at the reception desk. "Thief!" he exclaimed.

"Excuse me, what?" Emma put down the papers she had been holding to gift him with her full attention.

"Your housekeeper! Money was stolen out of my room!"

"All right, slow down, explain to me what happened."

"I had five hundred dollars in my room! Can you understand how much that is? Five hundred! And now it's just gone!"

"Was it in the safe?" Emma asked.

"Noo—"

"The hotel safes are there for your protection as well as ours." She had rehearsed that sentence as a child, knowing one day she might need it. "My Mom isn't here right now, but I will go inform her as soon as she gets back and she can ask Maria, our housekeeper, but I know Maria. She has been working here since I was born and we never had even one complaint." Emma sighed. "It's probably best if you call the police and report a burglary. That's our hotel policy."

"No." he answered right away. "No police."

Emma raised an eyebrow. "You have a problem with the police?"

Zach imagined the police questioning his mother, and then his mother questioning him. Where had he gotten five hundred dollars? She might even let the police cart him off, considering she couldn't deal with him.

"No, no problem. No need to tell your Mom or call the cops. Maybe I just misplaced the money. I'll go back and take another look. Maybe it'll turn up."

"Five hundred dollars is a lot of money," Emma commented. "Let me know if you don't find it and I

151

could inform the police for you. I would be happy to do that."

"All right. I will let you know." Zach fled the reception area, already grieving over those Nintendo games.

Cleo marched up the mountain, a woman on a mission, trying to keep her anger close so she didn't have to think of avalanches and white death.

"Where are you going?"

Cleona startled and turned around. An odd potpourri of people had set up camp just outside the fence surrounding Lucia's property. Colorful alpine two man tents, large canopies for communal cooking and dining, and various tee-pees. The most residents of this makeshift village looked eligible for membership in the AARP. Some were shoveling around the tents, others were hanging up clothes on a clothesline. They seemed to be settling in. A woman with flowing golden hair, markedly younger than the rest, took a step towards Cleona.

"Are you the welcoming committee?" Cleo asked.

"Do not enter the house of that damned woman!" She pointed to Lucia's house.

"I guess not then." There was a blond man behind the woman who was the size of a grizzly bear and looked as if maybe he had the IQ of an icicle. Behind them the group of senior citizens started congregating, reminding Cleo of escapees from One Flow Over The Cuckoo's Nest. Cleo's 'crazy' alarm bells were going off. She took a step back. "Who are you?"

"We are the Children of the Snowflake. I am High Priestess, Astra. Are you looking for guidance for your lost soul?"

"Not really," Cleo said.

"You are welcome to join us. I will show you the way."

"Way to what?"

"Enlightenment of course. The way to serenity. Those mittens—" she gestured to Cleona's puffy red Antarctica mittens that didn't match the rest of her outfit, "—may keep your hands warm but what will keep your soul warm?"

Cleona hid her mittens under her arms. "Thanks but no thanks."

"You are a fool if you think you don't need guidance. Ignorant." She opened her arms and rolled her eyes skyward.

"Astra! It's snowing!" shouted the Yeti behind her. He stuck out his tongue to sample a couple flakes, confirming Cleo's opinion of his IQ.

"From a clear sky!" Astra turned and addressed her flock. "It's a sign, my children! A sign from God!"

"Actually," Cleo couldn't help herself, "it's a meteorological phenomenon involving an uplift. Snowflakes form very high in the atmosphere and it can take some time before they reach the surface of the earth. The clouds that actually produced these snowflakes can already be long gone. The layman's term for snow falling from a clear sky is 'diamond dust', which does sound beautiful but is monetarily worthless."

"A sign, I said!" Astra hissed through clenched teeth.

"As you like." Cleo gave her a small bow and started towards Lucia's house.

"You soul is poisoned with facts!" Astra shouted after her. "You must have faith in something!"

Cleo turned around one last time and grinned. "Oh but I do have faith in something. I have faith that you're a nut."

Astra's face turned an amazing shade of red as she watched Cleo march away through the snow.

Lucia was pouring her morning coffee when the pounding on the door startled her. A couple drops splashed on the table. She sighed and wiped it up with the hem of her housedress.

"It's 'High Season' around here," Lucia remarked to Sparky. "We haven't had this many visitors since—" she trailed off. They had never had this many visitors.

She opened the door to Cleo's sour face. "That was quite the art project you concocted."

"Not good watch dog you are," Lucia chided Sparky. "No even bark!" She turned to Cleo. "You sow, you reap. But not fair to make nice boy steal for you."

"Nice boy, ha! He is a network of dour hormones held together by a layer of pimply skin. Not to mention it was his idea! I wouldn't have had to take him up on his offer if you had accepted my deal in the first place," she countered. "I made you a fantastic offer for that piece of rock! You should have taken it."

Lucia surveyed Cleo from head to toe, then nodded as if satisfied. "You want coffee?"

Cleo smiled, sensing a chance. "Yes, please." Lucia moved aside and Cleona stepped in.

It took her eyes a moment to adjust to the combination of glare and dimness. The room itself was dark but there were three windows where light of the highest quality poured in. It seemed a combination dining room and living room, with a tiny kitchen attached. There was no sofa and no television, but there was a fireplace blackened from use.

Cleo sat in an uncomfortable folding chair. The smell of coffee permeated the entire cabin. Lucia used an Italian percolator, warmed on the fire until water shot up through the coffee grounds. She poured a cup for Cleo. "Soon I must go to town for shopping," she said. "So many visitors! Not enough drink."

They sat across from each other behind cups of steaming coffee. The sun though the window lit up Lucia's face like a half-moon. Her skin appeared paper thin but practically wrinkle free. Cleona finally broke the silence. "Who are all those strange people I passed on the way here camping out near your house?"

"That angel with boots she say Children of the Snowflake. They want meteorite."

"They seem a bit kooky."

"Cookie?" Lucia looked puzzled.

"Crazy." Cleo wrapped her fingers around the mug, which had once probably been white. "You have aged very well," she observed, changing the subject.

Lucia laughed and sprayed a bit of coffee. "Compared to what? Meteorite? Why you say this? You only interested in old things."

"It's just an observation. That's my job; observation is the first step of the scientific method. I mean you don't look like you're twenty, thirty or even forty. But it is very difficult for me to try and guess your age. It must be difficult for people to live in these inhospitable mountains, always in constant struggle with nature. But you don't show it. I think you and I got off on the wrong foot and I apologize for that."

"Is ok." Lucia took a swallow from her mug. "Maybe you think I look good because I have meteorite and you don't. And maybe this true."

"How anyone actually looks is only perception, Miss Lucia, yours, mine or someone else's." Cleo took a sip and grimaced. "Do you have any milk?"

Lucia fetched a glass bottle from the cool box and poured a little in Cleona's cup. She took a sip. "I have never tasted milk like this before. What is it?"

"Milk straight from cow tit."

"Oh." Cleo put her cup down. "I've read reports about the mountain air. Most people think it's cleaner and healthier than air closer to sea level. But because of human activities, for example the cold starting of car motors, valleys in the mountains can be as vulnerable to pollution as coasts crawling with tourists. What do you think?"

"Maybe is right," Lucia agreed. "I never visit sea. Only part of sea I have I gave to you in art project." She winked.

"Time runs faster up here than it does at sea level," Cleo continued. "The farther from sea level you are the faster time flows. Pilots and flight attendants age faster than people with other jobs. You are actually aging faster than someone living close to the ocean. It has to do with the laws of physics."

"Well, I don't know what about that. My clock faster but I am happy. Me and Sparky here." She ruffled the dog between his ears.

"Did you know that your Matterhorn is actually African?" Cleona pretended to sip her coffee. "It travelled across on a tectonic plate and smashed into Europe."

Lucia laughed and slapped her knees. "Mountain is immigrant? Travel on a plate? Think I will never understand you, Science Lady. You full of crazy facts."

"Speaking of facts, can I ask you where you got this?" Cleo pulled the crystal out of her pocket and laid it on the table.

"That mine?"

"I found it in your art project."

"I don't remember." Lucia turned it over in her hands. "This maybe mountain crystal, lots around here." She handed it back to Cleo. "Don't remember this crystal. Maybe is mine, maybe not. Maybe is boy's."

Cleo pocketed it again. "I know you have every reason to say no now, especially after what I've done, but would you please consider letting me slice off a small piece of the meteor?"

"What for?"

"To study." Cleona leaned forward. "It's difficult for

me to explain, but this mission has become very personal for me."

"Personal?"

"Yes. I've sacrificed (Marc, she thought, and any chance of a normal life) a lot to turn my passion into my job, to get the funding I need to complete this mission. I look for organic molecules in extraterrestrial stone fragments. I look for the place where life began. This meteorite that you have is probably from a comet that came from outside our solar system—a comet that was behaving very strangely. I need to test it to be sure."

Lucia leaned back. "You look for God?"

Cleo flustered as she did at all religious references. She tapped her fingernails on the mug. "In a way, yes."

"I only go church for weddings, funerals and baptisms. Up here God is different. Up here God is all around."

"Does God include those lunatics camped outside?" They both laughed. Cleo decided not to tell Lucia that she was an atheist. "All I want is a small piece, Miss Lucia. If you give it to me, you can tell those crazies that I have it and they will leave you alone. Maybe they will come after me. I don't care. I am beyond caring. If I can make the discoveries that I think I can make with this meteorite, I will be as famous as Galileo or Newton."

Lucia studied Cleona. "You want to know where you come from."

"Not just me, Miss Lucia. All of us. Mankind."

"For me this not so important. No give rat's ass in a flying fire where I from. Most important is I'm here."

"If it doesn't mean so much to you, why won't you consider giving me a small piece?""

Lucia's face scrunched together as if she had been sucking on a lemon.

"You no understand. I no understand either. Maybe I forgot. But I make wish on falling star. I make wish, then I make promise. My wish, I don't know it anymore, but it came true, and so I keep my promise. The Promise Keeper. Keep safe and keep watch. Guardian of Memory." Lucia looked confused and Cleo wondered if she herself knew what she was talking about.

"Could I at least see it then?"

"The way you behave?" Lucia winked at her. "Only if you don't take it no more."

"I promise." Cleo hid her crossed fingers behind her back like a child.

"Ok then." Lucia left, spry for an old woman, and came back to the room with a towel in her hands. She passed it to Cleo. "Open it," she encouraged.

Cleo drew breath so sharply that it whistled. The rock inside was two things at once. It was everything she'd expected and nothing like she thought. It was solid and pitch black with crystals sprinkled all over it, and porous, a bit bigger than a football. It reminded Cleo of the Choc-o-lite candy bars from her childhood. She stroked it with one finger and shivered as she thought 'I am touching God'. Recce. Marc. Like Michelanglo's painting on the Sistine Chapel.

"Oh please Miss Lucia." Her gaze never wavered from her prize. "Can't I have just a small bit?"

Lucia snatched the rock back. "This not what you are looking for."

Cleo crossed her arms. So close and yet so far. The pull of the meteor was maddening. "Of course that is exactly what I am looking for! I came all this way, braving all this horrible snow. Did I mention that I am terrified of snow?"

"Terrified of snow?" Lucia raised one eyebrow.

"You aren't being logical," Cleona continued. "The meteor was not 'meant for you'. Anyone could have found it. It's just a rock from outer space, of no value to you. It's just coincidence that you found it."

"No coincidence."

"The definition of co-incidence are two things that happen at the same time. Every incident has its partner."

"Why you no find it then? Or Sister Snowflake?"

Cleo's frustration leveled up a notch. She looked into her coffee cup and saw chunks of milk floating around in it.

"I asked her same question already too," Lucia said proudly. "She have no answer."

"You have no idea what I have sacrificed to try and find this particular meteorite. This search has cost me some fingers and some toes." She held up her deformed hand. "It's just luck that you found it, that's all."

"Found it?" Lucia threw her head back and laughed. Her dentures clicked together. Sparky grunted. "It bynear knock me down, ay, Sparky?" Lucia placed it gingerly on the window sill. "Anyway, no deals. My piece of the sky and I am keeper. I make wish, and my wish come true!" She took the two coffee cups to the sink. "Now I keep my promise."

"Promise to whom?"

"I forgot."

"It's a myth, you know." Cleo said. "That you can wish on falling stars. It's just a story."

"No it's true. My uncle tell me. My Uncle—." But she had forgotten his name. She turned to look at Cleo, rinsing the coffee mugs out without looking at them. "I no want lose my wish."

"You don't even remember what you wished for!"

"No matter. Still a wish."

Cleo grinned sourly and shook her head. The image of pushing Lucia down, kicking the dog and snatching the meteorite crossed her mind again, and this time it was not so easy to get rid of.

"I know you think I a crazy old lady, but I not. I know for sure that if I give you, or anyone, my meteorite, I lose my wish."

Cleona pressed her hands together. "Wishes are for cheaters anyway. If you want something, like a trip to Africa for example, you make it into a goal. You work, you save, you plan, you carry out. That's how you get a trip to Africa, a diamond, a family, a Mercedes! Wishes are for lazy people trying to take short cuts."

Lucia laughed. "But you just say that Africa come to me on a plate! If this no magic, what is?" She turned back to her dishes. "Wishes are last bit of magic left in world."

Cleo stood up to leave. She was at the limit of her politeness.

"Why you want rock anyway?" Lucia asked. "What make it so special?"

"Miss Lucia, I believe the meteorite you found has indictations of nucleopeptides, the building blocks of life. Like I said, I want to test it for organic molecules. If I find anything, I promise to name it after you."

"Missy, better off look for life in your own heart." Lucia started drying the mugs. "Lucia is not great name for organic molecules. Whatever that be. Irma is better name. Or Fred." She laughed at her own joke.

"I hope you change your mind," Cleona said as she left. "Please, think about it."

As she hiked back down the mountain to the jeers of the Snowflake Children, Cleona asked herself the same question—why did she want the meteor? Nucleopeptides, physics-defying movement and organic molecules aside, there was another reason.

The meteor was still a connection to Marc.

Chapter 10

B efore Lucia opened her eyes, she listened. The sound that had awoken her was one she rarely heard, Sparky's low growl, accompanied by a strange rhythmic tapping that she couldn't place as one of her typical household noises. She sat up and it took her a moment for her eyes to adjust to the darkness and to locate him. He was crouched in the corner, his teeth glinting in the moonlight. His stare was locked on the window. Lucia followed his gaze and shrieked. Her bladder let go in a wet rush.

There was a grinning skull at the window. Grinning and tapping its raw finger bone on the glass. Lucia's hand crawled along the bedsheet for the rifle that she kept next to her bed. She didn't want to let the skull out of her sight, lest it somehow walk through the wall into her bedroom. She couldn't locate the rifle with her increasingly desperate fingers. She had to look away from the horrific apparition to find it. She moaned, low with fear, as she grabbed the rifle, sure that the skeleton would now be in her room, reaching out to her with its bony hands.

But it wasn't. And she saw that it wasn't a skeleton after all. It was Astra, with the moon behind her. She was smiling though, and still tapping her fingernail on the glass.

In the motion of a much younger woman, Lucia swung the rifle on her shoulder and levelled it at Astra. Astra wiggled her finger back and forth, still grinning, in a chiding gesture. Then Lucia blew a hole through her.

Or so she thought.

She rushed forward into the cold air with Sparky barking wildly, but there was no body in front of the shattered window. She looked towards the camp and Astra was standing over by the tents, 20 meters away, behind the fence. The whole crew was there, lit up by the moonlight, fires burning in the background. They were staring at her silently, not moving.

"Leave me alone! Go away!" she cried, but the night was still as twenty-odd pairs of eyes locked on her in mute judgement.

Lucia tacked up a pillowcase over the hole where the window had been, but didn't sleep for the rest of the night.

Reginald passed through the Mountaineers' Cemetery gates, his fingers working the latch with some difficulty. For a brief second he imagined Viet Cong hiding behind the larger headstones. But the graveyard was empty and deceased were silent. There were no auras, only the white and grey of the world before the sun has risen and everything fills with colours. The sun was on its way but the cemetery was permanently in the Matterhorn's shadow, which Reginald found fitting. The mountain that had held so much influence over these climbers lives also dominated their final places of rest. The tourists were probably just starting their breakfasts, ordering their lattes and buttering their toast, so Reginald was alone with the dead.

Those buried in this cemetery shared one thing in common, Reginald thought as he walked down the path. In life they had possessed that crazy sparkle in their eyes—the captured light from the top of the Matterhorn, and some unfathomable need to climb it. It would take a very unusual kind of person, Reginald mused, to want to scale that phantasmagorical mountain that looked as if it belonged on another planet—a mountain with pitiless ridges and an unforgiving heart of ice. He had seen soldiers with that same glint in their eyes--soldiers that sprinted through minefields, dodged enemy bullets coming from bushes, ran down beaches as bombs rained from the sky. There were other cemeteries full of these soldiers, people simply incapable of living out their natural lifespans. Like mountain climbers.

When George Mallory was asked why he wanted to climb Mount Everest, he answered: "Because it's there."—the three most famous words in mountaineering. Reginald imagined that those buried here had shared the same sentiment, although he personally failed to understand it. It seemed like a stupid reason to risk one's life.

Some of the gravestones were upright, and some horizontal. But even those lying down were free of snow, as if they were warm. The walkways had already been shovelled, probably by a dedicated caretaker in the shadows before dawn. There was a great difference among the apparent cost of the headstones.

Some were elaborate and decorated with tools of the climbing trade—hiking sticks, carabiners. Some were plain, and some were only wooden crosses. Some had the cause of death listed on the marker: avalanche, a rockfall, a crevasse. So many ways to die on the Matterhorn. There was one simply inscribed: I Chose to Climb with a red pickaxe and an American flag draped around like a frozen cape.

Reginald found his dad in the northwest corner of the cemetery. "Closest to home," he noted. He knelt down and his knees cracked like gunshots. At last, he had found this man who he barely remembered. "Hello, Dad. It's been a while. As a matter of fact, it's been a lifetime, my lifetime."

He took a deep breath. "There are a lot of questions I never got to ask you. If you have a story you wanted to tell me before you left. What you remember about your own mother and father, or your grandparents." He leaned forward. "And I always wanted to ask you--why did you leave us, Dad? Was climbing the Matterhorn really more important than a lifetime with me? Than growing old with Mom? Do you regret it?"

He traced the letters on the headstone with his finger—William Patterson. Suddenly the door to all those blocked memories of his father flooded in: riding on his father's strong shoulders watching the 4th of July parade and waving a tiny flag, going fishing and getting water into his long rubber boats, losing countless games of chess, soaking the stamps from letters to place carefully in an album, eating dinner together with his beautiful, laughing mother and his father with mischief in his eyes. That glint he had, the glint of a daredevil soldier, of a mountaineer.

He realized that his father had had no choice. It was in his DNA.

Don't think you're any better than your father, the Dark Soldier whispered. In some ways you are the same. You did a miserable job teaching Peggy to drive and she slammed into a brick wall. The autopsy revealed that she was pregnant--carrying the child you never had. And where were you? Off fighting someone else's war in Vietnam. You aren't any better than your father was. That's why you couldn't remember him. He was the part of yourself that you wanted to forget.

Reginald stood up and his knees cracked again. He hated that Dark Soldier. He took the picture from his jacket pocket--the one of his father up on the mountain, sunglasses hiding those resolute eyes with the maniacal glint.

"I can't forgive myself, Dad. But I can forgive you."

He laid the picture of his father on the grave and covered it with a small stone. He stood there for a long time, until the tourists and skiers started coming out of the nests to enjoy a beautiful day in the mountains.

Amanda, Zach and Cleona were eating their meals, but none of them was enjoying the food. Cleo was doing her best to avoid eye contact with her dinner companions. A stiff and graceless silence eddied between them, and the noise of silverware clinking against the plates and their own chewing filled their ears.

Amanda had believed that Zach had reached peak grumpiness long ago, but she was wrong. She snuck glances at him. He was slumped low in his chair, eyes under heavy lids, as if he were looking out from some dark place instead from across the table. His contemptuous stare was locked on Cleona who wasn't even looking up from her salad.

Reginald was sitting at his table across the room, making a list which of his possessions should go to which charities after he was dead. He was occasionally lifting a fork full of salad to his mouth in a perfect right angle.

Vera Buxomberger was sitting alone, dressed in a royal blue tent dress and wearing makeup that looked as though it had been applied with a spatula. She was discussing something in hushed tones with the salt shaker.

Except for Emma bopping in and out, they were the only people in the dining room.

After Emma cleared the salad bowl, Cleona started plugging numbers into the formula $N(>D)=37D$ squared by -2.7, the power-law distribution at which the earth receives meteors. She was making her calculations in blue felt pen on the pristine white tablecloth. Emma had passed by several times, frowning, but Cleona didn't notice her. She was lost in a stellar cloud of mathematics. Finally Emma brought the fish course, placing Cleona's plate over her equations. Cleo promptly began to dissect the fish.

Zach grunted and took out his cellphone. The fish stared at him with dead eyes, its mouth open in what appeared to be shock. He took a picture of it. Amanda picked at the fish with her fork and took a deep swig of wine.

There were several text messages for Zach from Anson back home in Ohio. Anson was giving him a play-by-play of classmate Chloe's end-of-vacation party and sending him photos of drunken girls, smiling, sticking their tongues out, pouting. Zach sent him the picture of the dead fish.

Amanda forced herself to take a bite of fish around a lump in her throat, picked out a small bone from between the teeth, inhaled deeply. She felt compelled to break the deafening silence. She asked the first question she could think of: "What is the strangest thing that ever happened to you?"

Cleona put down her fork, startled at the interruption. "Pardon?"

"You know, something from the Twilight Zone." She took another sip of wine. "I saw a ghost once. Actually I never saw it at all but I'm sure it was there. I was babysitting at the time. I must have been around fourteen. I had been watching MTV, we didn't have it at home so I actually looked forward to babysitting. Then I noticed the little girl, Maria, was not in the living room playing with her Barbies anymore. I called after her but she didn't answer. I started to get frantic, you know, she was my responsibility and all. I was so relieved when I found her on the stairs, staring off into space.

'Maria, you scared me! You have to tell me the next time before you disappear.'

She didn't even look at me. 'Who's that lady with the braid?'

'Which lady?'

She pointed to the space under the landing, to an empty wall. 'That lady.'

'Sweetie, there's no lady there.'

'Yes there is. She's making funny faces at me.' Maria scrunched her face up and stuck her tongue out. 'I don't like that braid lady.' I noticed then that Maria's bright eyes were full of tears.

'Come on, sweetie. Let's leave the braid lady alone and go get a snack.' I took Maria's hand and led her to the kitchen. She was really quiet and clingy for the rest of the afternoon. She sat on my lap and we watched MTV together.

When her mother got home I told her what had happened. The color drained from her face as she explained that the last owner, a woman, had hung herself in the house. They didn't live there much longer after that. They moved and I didn't get to sit for Maria again or watch MTV for a while." Amanda smiled inwardly, noticing that Zach had put his phone on the table and had been listening to her story. "Creepy, huh?" she asked him.

"You never told me that before," Zach said.

"I've never told anyone that before," Amanda answered. She rubbed her eye. It was itching and she hoped she wasn't getting an eye infection.

"I'm sure there's a logical explanation, though." Cleona said. "Maybe she had seen a hanging woman on television or overheard her parents talking about it."

"Maybe," Amanda consented. "But then again, maybe not."

"You don't believe in ghosts, then?" Zach asked Cleona. His tone was snarky.

"No, but – "The determined looked ebbed out of her eyes. She cleared her throat. "Someone once told me that comets are the ghosts of the galaxy. Their appearance is called an 'apparition'. Their purpose is a mystery." She took the crystal out of her pocket. Zach perked up. It was the same crystal that Lucia had planted in the fake meteor! "I have a mystery of my own. Maybe you can help me solve it."

"What are you doing with my crystal?"

They all looked up, startled, to see Reginald charging over to their table. He snatched it out of Cleona's fingers. "Where did you get this?" he demanded.

"Your crystal?" Cleona paled.

"Yes, mine! How did you get this? Where did you find it?"

Cleona turned to Zachary. "I thought, that Lucia said, it was yours—? Maybe you would like to shed some light on this dilemma?"

"I'm warning you, though, then everything comes out," Zach said.

"What do you mean? What's going on here?" Amanda demanded.

"Oh, I would love know that too!" They were all surprised when Lucia walked in, waggy-tail Sparky in tow. She pulled over a chair from another table and squeezed between Reginald and Cleona. "Look strange," she eyed the fish with interest. "Weird shape for meat."

"Miss Lucia!" Reginald's frown righted to a smile. He pocketed his crystal. "What are you doing here?"

"Well, since no one visit me yesterday, I thought I come to you instead!"

Zach slunk back in his chair.

"I change mind," Lucia continued. "You owe me favor," she nodded to Zach, "and you wish my treasure—" she nodded to Cleona, "what you want I don't know and you neither." She took Reginald's hand. "But I know I need help."

"What's the matter, Miss Lucia?" Reginald asked.

Lucia laid her wrinkled hand over his. "These Snowflake children. They no go. I afraid they hurt me."

"Who are you?" Amanda demanded. "How do you know my son?"

"Snowflake children?" Reginald squeezed her hand.

"You mean democrats?"

"Religious cultists," Cleona said. "I saw them myself yesterday."

"Snowflakes dear." Lucia patted his hand as if she were his wife of sixty years. "They make fire near my house and dance around but do not melt. They too want rock. Maybe they even try steal it, this wrong thing to do." She stared pointedly at Cleona.

Cleo cleared her throat. "Did you leave the meteor there alone?"

"Is few million years old, can probably be alone a few hours." Lucia cackled. "No worries, I hide treasure where they cannot find it. But I worry they try hurt me or Sparky. They act crazy. Dance at night, pray to strange gods and devils. Sparky also go crazy. I want them gone. I want my peace."

Reginald leaned forward. "How can we help you?"

"I don't know." Lucia looked disorientated, and age settled over her like a closing curtain. Amanda thought that there was nothing more tragic than an old woman. She had seen it often enough working in the nursing home. Looking lost in their own rooms. Appearing confused in a building they had lived in for years. You saw yourself in their eyes. Your future.

"I stop by police before I come to you but they nothing can do. Snowflakes are 'camping' on 'public land'. They put away even their garbage so I can no say they are littering!"

"Put enough snowflakes together and you get an avalanche," Zach muttered.

"Excuse me," Amanda reached forward and stopped short of touching the woman's elbow—keeping a measure of distance as a sign of respect. "You are Lucia Zurbriggen?"

"Yes."

"The lady from the picture? With the meteorite?"

"Yes."

"How do you know Zachary?"

"Why, the young sir paid me a visit the other night."

"What?" Amanda was relieved, so it wasn't drugs after all, but all the more curious. She looked at her son. "Do you know this lady?"

"Yeah. She—"he tilted his head towards Cleona

"asked me if I would break in and steal the meteorite. But I got caught."

"What?" Amanda demanded of Cleona.

Cleo shrugged. "It was his idea. I just took him up on it. And he still owes me 500 dollars because he and his new senior buddy made me a meteorite with sand and gum wrappers."

"I don't have the money anymore anyway," Zachary said. "The maid stole it."

"Of all the numbskull things you could have done, Zachary!" Amanda slapped the table and all the drinks jiggled. "Breaking and entering! Like we need anymore trouble with the law!" She turned to Lucia. "I want to apologize for the actions of my son. It was wrong of him to break into your house and try to steal what was yours." She glared at Cleo, who brushed at her shoulder as if flicking off Amanda's scorn like a flake of dandruff.

Lucia patted Amanda's hand. "He is not bad boy. He on the wrong path. Not even Cleona's fault."

"I guess this is yours then." Amanda took the 500 dollars out of her purse and pushed them across the table to Cleona.

"Mom!"

"Well it's just what you deserve, lying and trying to steal!"

Zach scowled. "Just make sure you put it back in the safe," he told Cleona. "Combination's 2-3-2-3 in case you forgot."

Cleona glared at him and pocketed her money.

Amanda turned to Lucia, who was glowing with

amusement. "What did you mean, you wanted to call him up on a favor?"

"I no call police. I keep secret. He say he 'owe me one'."

"Well, that deal's off," Zach said. "You just told everyone."

"What do you mean? I never tell. You told on yourself." She winked.

"What is it you need, Miss Lucia?" Reginald asked.

"Get rid of snowflakes. Need more than shovel." Lucia smiled and glanced dreamily at the ceiling. "Everyone love meteorite, it bring me trouble. But it also give me a wish."

"We've been over this territory," Cleo said briskly. "That's a legend, a myth. There are no 'wishes come true'."

"Do you know there used to be wolves in mountains?" Lucia asked.

"What has that got to do with anything?"

"Oh yes. I used to hear them howl at night."

"Miss Lucia, please stick to the subject."

Lucia laughed. "Lots of things give wishes. Birthday candles. Coins in fountains. Anyway, what you care? If you no believe in wishes, then you have none."

"She doesn't believe in ghosts either," Zach threw in.

Lucia beamed at him and turned to Cleona. "Anyway, you no more have to wish. If you help me with Snowflake problem, rock is yours."

Cleona's heart pounded hard. "Do you mean it? Of course I will!"

"Naturally I too will help the great lady," Reginald chimed in.

"Zach will help you too," Amanda said. "I'll make sure of it." She glared at her son, who rolled his eyes but reluctantly nodded.

In the corner of the room, Vera Buxomberger had put down her saltshaker and turned up her hearing aid.

Chapter 11

The dark deepened outside as they huddled around the tablecloth stained with equations and drink rings. Emma dimmed the lights and then joined them, occasionally bringing more water for the table or more wine for Amanda. The night pressed against the windows. Everyone forgot Vera in the corner.

"Maybe we can scare them away?" Zachary suggested. "I've already met your gun," he said to Lucia. "Up close and personal."

Amanda shook her head. "I'll be the voice of reason here." She took a gulp of wine. "It's too dangerous. Someone could accidentally get shot."

"We need to plan this like a military operation," Reginald said. "We have a goal—removal of these pests. We need a strategy, like in Vietnam."

"Yes, because we all know how successful that was." Cleo rolled her eyes. "What do you want to do, spray them with Agent Orange?"

Reginald stiffened.

"Could we somehow scare them without the gun?" Amanda suggested.

"Yes because we are a very scary bunch, especially you," Cleo commented.

"Well you seem to be good at playing Devil's Advocate, as well as contracting innocent teenagers to do your dirty work, but not much else." Amanda crossed her arms. "Why don't you come up with a plan?"

"'Innocent teenager'? Ha! That's a misnomer if I ever heard one!"

Lucia cackled. "I have Devil's Advocate, Voice of Reason and innocent teenager on my side."

"And GI Joe, don't forget," Zachary said. Reginald's scalp reddened under his wispy white hair.

"Maybe instead of a military operation, we could use the Scientific Method." Cleo ticked off her points on her fingers. "It's the way I solve all my problems. Observation: these fruit cakes want Lucia's meteorite. Hypothesis: They won't leave until they get it." Cleona leaned forward. "I think we should give them what they want."

"What you mean?" Lucia exclaimed. "You steal and lie for holy rock, then you give away?"

"I would do that maybe, if the leader of that cult was able to pry it out of my dead hands. I mean, we should give them what they think they want. Or what they think is what they want."

"What?" Emma asked.

"Huh?" Zachary asked.

Cleo turned to Lucia. "You aren't the only one who can make a pretty mean fake meteor. At least mine might even look real." She leaned back, folded her hands behind her head and smiled. "I have an idea."

28 hours later Lucia was back in her cabin, keeping to her normal routine and forcing herself to stay calm while her heart was leaping in her chest like Sparky

in the snow. Lucia's pocket watch put the hour at fourteen minutes after midnight. The air was heavy with the tension of something about to happen. The day was new. The possibilities were open.

She hadn't yet been able convince the village contractor to climb the mountain to replace the window, so she had set up a cot into the dining room. She kept her bedroom door closed. She glanced at it uneasily as she settled into bed, fully dressed. She had been able to keep tabs on Astra and her followers from her bedroom, but her living room window faced north. She had no idea what they were up to. It would be easy enough for one of them to creep in through the broken window. They could be making a bonfire out of her bed this very moment and she wouldn't even know.

The fire in the fireplace had burned down and the glow from the embers filled the little room. Even though Lucia had rolled up a sweater to block the draft from under the bedroom door, the cold was sneaking in. She could see her breath in front of her eyes, smoky orange in the dying firelight, as she stared at the ceiling. She tucked the edges of the blanket under her body to keep out the frozen air. Her feet tingled in spite of the two pairs of socks she was wearing.

She was thin enough that Sparky managed to squeeze onto the cot next to her. He wasn't permitted on her bed, but she figured she would make an exception with the cot. Just for warmth.

In spite of everything, Lucia wasn't afraid. She was

experiencing an emotion that she was unfamiliar with, and could finally place it as excitement, and a sense of being cared for. She hadn't felt that since her mother had died. Her stomach felt tickled from the inside. She and Sparky weren't alone with the crazies on the mountain tonight.

Lucia heard a loud bang overhead. "It's starting." She stroked Sparky's fur and got out of bed and put on her boots. She put the meteor in a backpack and hoisted it onto her shoulders. On the way out she noticed her skis, standing in the corner. She took one in her hand and the disturbed dust caused her to sneeze.

"It's been a while." She smiled and strapped the skis on. "I think it's time for some adventure."

Zachary, Reginald, Amanda, Emma and Cleona were hunched down behind the snow drift. The moon on the snow produced an unearthly blue glow that enabled them to see fairly well. Amanda felt conspicuous in her bright orange ski jacket. Reginald had wrinkled his nose when they had met in the hotel lobby, but it was the only jacket she had. The others were better prepared for espionage in their dark clothes. She felt like the only color in a black and white movie. "The stars are so pretty up here."

"We are on a mission, not a date," Cleona said. "But, just for your information, stars are more prominent in the mountains due to thinner air and less light pollution."

"How romantic." Amanda said.

Zach and Reginald crawled up the snow hill and

peeked over the top on the camp. "They're still there," Zach reported. He waved the others to have a look.

"They must be batty," Reginald whispered. He shivered. "My old bones are telling me that it's fifty below outside. They are walking around in floaty scarves and bed sheets!"

Astra had set up a camp that looked like a small city. There were three bonfires lit, one in the middle of the tents and one on each side. The group had set up white-colored mountain climbing tents, the kind alpinists slept in at high altitudes. Zachary had once seen a documentary about a Himalayan trek where those tents were used. "Batshit bonkers," he agreed. They slid back down the drift.

"Insanity keeps you warm," Cleo brushed loose snow from her pants. "That might be a hypothesis worth testing."

"Well, they may not be completely insane," Emma pointed out. "They are wearing boots."

Cleo nodded. "Good observation, young lady. And are we ready to blow them out of their boots?"

They all nodded solemnly.

"I haven't done anything like this since I retired from the Army," Reginald commented, clapping Zachary on the back. "You aim long and low, son. Right over their camp."

Amanda noticed that Zach didn't wince at being touched. "Can you please now tell me what the plan is?" She wished she hadn't gotten so sloshed yesterday that she had needed to go to bed and missed the plotting part of the mission. Cleo had told her this morning in a condescending tone that she didn't need her help, but Amanda wasn't in the mood to be talked down to, especially by a woman who had contracted her son to commit a crime. There was no way she was leaving Zach and Cleo alone to do any more questionable deeds. It was her neck too, and she couldn't afford to have the police involved.

Zach winked at her. "These nutty people are looking for shooting stars. We are going to give them some."

"What?"

"Fireworks, Mz. Bennett," Emma said. "I found some leftover from the Swiss National Holiday celebration in the cellar of the hotel. We do a big show in August, but it rained last year so we didn't bother to set everything off." She jammed the firing tube into the snow. "The tube is actually not designed to be fired sideways, only straight up. We'll have to pack it in a bit."

"Let's leave the fuse out though, so I can light it," Zach said. He pulled his glove off with his teeth wrapped the fuse in a plastic bag so it wouldn't get wet. He knelt beside Emma and helped her pack snow around the tube.

The goofy grin felt fine on Amanda's face as she watched them work. Just fine. She was even forgetting that she was freezing. "How do you know about fireworks?"

"We set some off at Dad's house last Fourth of July weekend."

"Oh." Amanda remembered that lonely fourth. She

had spent the holiday alone. That had been before the accident. She shivered in her jacket.

"I planted a fake meteor behind the opposite snowbank," Cleo pointed. "I'm going to sneak around and light the coal I put on the ground, make it look like it just landed. I sprinkled it with sulfur too, so it stinks. You and Lucia aren't the only ones who can organize a fake meteorite." She looked pointedly at Zach. "And mine is much better because it's not made of dishtowels and gum wrappers and Elmer's glue and sand. And mine is organic. And vegan."

Zach gave her a thumbs up.

"All right then Sargent Skye you go ahead on over and light it up," Reginald directed. "How long do you need?"

"Ten minutes to sneak around the camp with a wide enough berth. Once the stuff is lit it burns for half an hour so we have a huge time window."

"Good. You know what to do. After you light it go back to the hotel. We'll set off the fireworks show. Then we'll wait here until those people go investigate and after that we will sneak down ourselves."

"I can send Zach a text message when I'm finished," Cleona said. "Then you will know when to set the fireworks off."

Reginald gave her a short nod. "Good idea."

"Roger, Colonel Imaginary Hat. See you back at the hotel." Cleona saluted and tramped away through the snow. So much snow. At night. But Cleo had forgotten to be scared.

Reginald put his hands on his hips. "What did she call me?"

"Colonel Imaginary Hat," Zach answered.

"Why does she refer to me that way?" Reginald touched the hat on his head. "My hat is real."

"No idea," Amanda said. Zachary grinned.

"Shouldn't one of us go check on Lucia? After we set it off?" Emma asked.

"I wouldn't worry too much about her," Zachary said. 'She's really got that 'Wise Old Lady of the Mountains' thing going on."

"No need to worry at all," Reginald said. "We will meet Lucia later in the hotel lobby. Here." He handed Emma a small whisk broom. "You come down last. Backward. Wipe our footprints away as you walk. You won't be able to eradicate them all, but at least disguise them as best you can."

Emma smiled and saluted. She looked adorable in her rose-colored snow hat. Amanda noticed Zach notice. He wore a dopey grin when he looked at Emma. Please, God, she prayed silently. I'm not religious but let the dark times be over. Please let them be over. Haven't we suffered enough? I want my son back—the way he was before the accident. Please let this good deed pay off the bad debts. I'll try and be a better mom. Thank you. Amen.

Reginald kept an eagle eye on his stopwatch and when ten minutes had passed he nodded to Zach. Zach searched his pockets, at first meticulously, then ever more frantically. "I don't have the lighter."

"What?" Emma hissed.

"Go through your pockets again. Take your time," Reginald advised.

"Yes honey. I'm sure it just worked its way into the corner of one of your pockets. Check again," Amanda pleaded. She found all kinds of things in the corners of his pants pocket when doing the laundry.

His worried eyes shone in the moonlight as his fingers came up empty. "No. It's gone."

They stared at each other. "Now what?" Emma asked.

Then Amanda said, "Wait."

She unzipped her ski jacket and reached into the inner pocket, the one designed for cell phones and sunglasses, and pulled out a matchbook. She flicked it open. Four matches left.

"Mom I love you!" Zach gave her a squeeze.

"Good thing I didn't wash the jacket! They are from the time we went camping in autumn, remember? When it was so cold. We made hot dogs over the campfire." That, too, was before the accident. Before innocence lost.

"I remember," Zach said. He checked his phone. "Cleo's all set."

"Good. Then light her up." Reginald clapped his hands together.

The first match lit on the first try. The flame wobbled a bit, fighting for life in the bitter cold. Zach eased down and lit the fuse. They all hurried behind the tube and watched as blue fire exploded over the sky over the camp. There was even a loud explosion.

"I put some firecrackers in there too," Emma explained.

They climbed the drift and watched with amusement as the cult members scampered in the direction of the fireworks.

"All right. Let's go," Reginald said.

Astra dashed in the direction that the lights in the sky had fallen, her heart thudding inside her slim rib cage. Her brother bumbled behind her, and the rest of the Snowflake Children were shuffling, ambling and limping behind. Astra was the most agile of the bunch, mentally and physically, and that's the way she preferred it. She wanted to be first to see whatever had just torn through the sky. Had God actually granted her wish? That was impossible, she chided herself. She had never admitted to anyone that she was an atheist.

She peered over the snow bank. It was difficult to classify it as anything other than a miracle. The snow was glowing and little fires burned along black streaks. She had never seen snow burn before. There was a charred hole where something had crashed. Her brother gasped behind her.

"Oh wow," she whispered in awe. She slid down the snow bank, getting snow in her furry boots. The smell of rotten eggs intensified as she got closer. Was it from outer space? Was the universe so putrid?

She bent down over the hole. The rock was pitch black in color, peppered with holes where strange air had once bubbled. The edges looked worn, as if eroded by water. She touched it with wonder and snapped her hand back. Hot. Astra's mouth was filled with the taste of sulfur. She spit on the ground, causing the snow to sizzle.

Something was wrong here. The scene was a little too perfect. Although she had no experience, she imagined that meteorite crashes were sloppy affairs. This looked more like a scene from a movie set. The track was perfectly straight. The burning snow framed the stage. The Snowflakes were ooh-ing and ahh-ing behind her and her brother was burbling some sort of excited nonsense like a retarded word fountain but Astra wasn't convinced the find was real. Something nibbled at the corner of her brain and she had learned long ago to trust her instincts. But it was a challenge to examine anything with only the blue glow of the snow and the quickly fading embers of the crash for illumination.

"Bring me a torch, brotherheart," she ordered. "I want to have a look at this miracle."

He shuffled away obediently. She tried to herd her followers like a border collie herds spastic sheep, pointing at the heavens and promising extra celestrial points (these were the points needed to get into heaven) for the first person to locate another shooting star, trying to keep their attention skywards that they wouldn't trample over the scene. It was like trying to collect milk in a basket. She should have sent old Olaf with his bad knee and artifical hip to get the torch. Olaf would have been faster than her beloved brotherheart.

Rufus finally arrived dripping sparks. Astra positioned him in front of the herd and relieved him of his torch, investigating the scene by herself.

The torch threw shadowed licks of light over the

crash site. Carefully skirting the burning snow skid marks on her way to examine the rock, she noticed something red sticking out of the snow. Astra yanked it out. A red mitten, designed for especially arctic (or Antarctic) temperatures. And Astra remembered where she had seen that red mitten before.

"Oh, you," she said almost lovingly. Her sanity had been walking the tight edge of a cliff for a long time now, and it was almost a relief as it tumbled over. The vengeful and powerful Priestess of Snow had been betrayed.

It is the little things that start an avalanche—a foot step, a bird song. A poorly played trick. Small incidents—some innocent, some not so. But once the avalanche began, white death roared down and destroyed everything in its path.

Reginald, Amanda, Zach and Emma creeped around the tents down the mountain, stepping in each other's footprints before Emma brushed them away. Reginald glanced back. The mountain was alive with excitement. There were happy shouts from the cult members and Reginald fleetingly thought of Lucia, hoping she was all right in the flurry. Maybe Emma was right, they should have checked on her.

He needn't have worried.

They wound their way down the trail and back into the village, trying to act as casual as possible for such a motley group on the move after midnight on a weekday. Their shared secret pulled them together like a magnetic force, connecting them without being seen. They got back to the hotel, stomping the snow off their boots. Cleona, Lucia and Sparky were waiting in the reception area, along with Claudia Andermatt, arms crossed and tapping her foot. Askia, the hotel dog, was cuddled up next to Sparky, who looked pleased with himself.

"Where have you been young lady?" she demanded of Emma.

Emma grabbed Zach's hand, surprising him. "Sorry. Mum, we were on a walk."

"You should have told me. I was worried sick. Fortunately Doctor Skye said that you were on your way home, or I would have called the police!" She drummed her perfectly lacquered fingernails on the counter. "Well say goodnight to the guests now and get along to bed. You have to man the reception desk tomorrow. Good night to the rest of you as well." She gave a polite small bow and took her leave.

"Thanks for covering for me." Emma squeezed his hand in thanks.

"My pleasure." He tried and failed to stop the foolish grin from spreading across his face.

"And you too," she said to Cleona.

"We couldn't have done it without you," Cleo said. "Now if you forget about the ruined tablecloth, we're even."

She nodded. "See you tomorrow." She stretched up and gave Zach a quick kiss on the corner of his lips and left with a wave.

"Yeah, see you." His eyes followed her every movement as she walked down the hall.

"You look like you've been hit by a sledgehammer," Cleona observed.

Zach blushed.

"I thank you all for helping me," Lucia said to them. "I sleep better now."

"You can sleep in my room tonight," Cleona said. "You don't have to walk back up the mountain. I have a double bed. Tomorrow we can go with you to make sure they're gone."

"Or you are welcome in my room," Reginald offered.

"Offers. Offers. Which one to pick?" Lucia smiled.

Amanda was about to add something to the conversation when a ghost charging up the hill towards the hotel grabbed her attention. Frozen fear sizzled through her like cold electricity. "Something's coming." She pointed a trembling finger at the glass door behind Lucia.

"Oh shit it's that crazy bitch," Zach said.

"And she doesn't look pleased," Cleo observed.

Astra burst into the lobby and Lucia cringed away, instinctively holding the meteorite against her body.

"Youuuuuuuu-" Astra screamed, and something sharp and silver slid out of her sleeve into her fist.

"Watch out she has a knife!" Amanda warned. Astra lurched forward and shoved the knife into Lucia's chest. Lucia stumbled back, a glut of blood shot from her mouth, and the meteor crashed to the floor. Astra darted forward to grab it. Reginald tried to catch Lucia but she crumpled to the floor at the same time Zach tackled Astra the way he had learned in football practice.

"Call an ambulance!" Amanda shouted. She knelt beside Lucia.

Astra twisted and writhed in Zach's grip. "You people are from Satan! You tried to trick me and the Good Flock! You will all roast in hell!" She broke free and ran right through the lobby door, shattered glass scattering everywhere.

Zach started after her but Claudia's hand fell on his arm. "Better leave that for the police." She was holding a telephone in her other hand and said something into the receiver in German.

Reginald also knelt, with some difficulty, next to Lucia. He searched her face for something of Private Miller's, listened for some cryptic message, but Lucia just groaned. "Keep as still as possible," he advised, stroking her cheek.

Even in the urgency of the situation, Amanda noticed the tender way Reginald touched the old woman. She tried to remember her first aid training from the nursing home but only called up images of bedpans and pureed peas.

Cleona couldn't believe her luck! Here it was, the object that she had coveted, the bounty of her quest, the thing she would have sold her soul for. But after the initial wave of triumph and success, she felt a yawning emptiness as she regarded the ordinary-looking rock. She didn't have Marc back, and who really cared if there was life outside the solar system? Who really cared? The life and death drama unfolding in front of her was more urgent. Reginald wore the look of a wounded puppy and Amanda was wringing her hands as if she could squeeze assistance from them. Cleona sighed. With a conscious effort, she withdrew her attention from the meteorite and rushed to Lucia's side, kneeling down in the expanding pool. Blood had turned the melting snow pink.

She found a pulse throbbing delicately in the old woman's neck. She unbuttoned the tattered blue coat. "Lucia can you hear me? I'm going to put you in the resting position." She grabbed the old woman's shoulder and under her bony hip and turned her on her side. Lucia moaned and her eyes fluttered.

"Her mouth should be slightly open." Reginald's training was coming back to him. Cleona dutifully eased Lucia's jaw down and examined the knife buried in the old woman's chest. "Don't take that out!" Reginald warned.

"I wasn't considering it," Cleona said evenly.

Lucia's breaths came in labored gasps and something in her lungs was whistling. Then her eyes eased open. "Nicht so. So will ich nicht sterben."

"What did she say?" Amanda asked Claudia.

Claudia's gaze was fixed on Lucia. "She said that she doesn't want to die like this."

Sparky and Askia were whining in unison.

"Oh Miss Lucia," Reginald comforted. "It's not your time yet."

Lucia eyes flew open. She reached out and grabbed Reginald's sleeve. "Have you ever loved?" Then she fainted.

A minute later the paramedics arrived.

Chapter 12

She remembered. In the darkness, shards of her life flew together to make a mosaic.

Lucia had spent her entire life in the mountains—in the valley that only provided one slice of sky. The children of Zermatt were used to that. The valley was their universe. Sometimes there were whispers of wars or financial crises in the outside world but not even the news reached them when the weather was bad. Lucia's Zermatt, before it grew thick with tourists, was an isolated village almost unreachable for visitors, a community existing at the outer reaches of the civilized world. The residents still carried a piece of the isolation inside themselves—their hooded eyes regarded strangers mistrustfully. Her Uncle Bruno used to pound his chest and proclaim that they lived at the top of the world with God as their neighbor.

Lucia was a summertime baby, so it was deep winter when she first started to become aware of her environment. She recognized that the mountains and the clouds matched in color. They reflected each other and existed in harmony. When the mountains were serene white the clouds were white and when the clouds were dream-like smoky blue and pink the mountains were too. When the sky turned angry grey the mountains darkened and became less forgiving of navigational errors. Lucia's sky and Lucia's land and Lucia's whole world were lorded over by the Matterhorn. When she was older, her Uncle Bruno once told her that the Matterhorn was a big birthday candle lit on top just for her.

"But it's not my birthday," Lucia would protest.

"The mountain does not know that," her uncle reassured her, tugging one of her blonde braids. "Don't forget your wish."

Young Lucia never shook the idea that the mountain ignited just for her. On the overcast days it failed to light, but the sunny ones more than made up for it. It burned red at sunrise and pink gold at sunset. She didn't see the pink gold often but in winter the sun's arc though the sky was smaller and offered her this special treat. She would often turn to the Matterhorn during her daily chores without thinking about it— her light, her anchor.

Lucia also had a name for all the winds. There was the naughty October wind which stole her best Sunday hat on the way to church one morning, and the killer January wind. There was the strange warm wind that blew from the South in April, bending around her precious Matterhorn, turning the sky orange and sending melted snow cascading down the mountain in waterfalls. The South, beyond the Italian Alps, was something Lucia could not even imagine. Uncle Bruno told her that summer reigned there all year round.

Uncle Bruno! Filled with stories and philosophy— he came rolling back in her memory— he had a generous stomach which jiggled when he laughed. She remembered him telling about glaciers that devoured houses, armies of elephants marching around the mountains, how it felt to touch the sky with his bare hands. He had dark eyes and dark hair and his beard was sprinkled with silver. Lucia's mother Hannelore often joked that there was some Italian blood in him. How could she have forgotten her much beloved Uncle Bruno?

How indeed?

She remembered how he had built a patio attachment for the cabin Lucia shared with her mother. He carried the stones for the floor up the mountain himself, sweat dripping from his beard. How they used to watch the clouds sail across the sky from that patio and try to find familiar shapes in them. There were special ones that formed over mountain peaks that were just as flared as her mother's Sunday dress. When they saw a particularly pretty one, Uncle Bruno would tell Lucia to fetch his sketchpad and he would try to capture it before the wind tore it apart. If he managed to get it outlined he could fill it in with his imagination. He even succeeded in depicting the way the light shone from within the cloud.

"One day we will climb to the top of the Matterhorn and touch its fire," Uncle Bruno promised.

But that day was never to come. When Lucia was seven, her uncle had what Hannelore called a 'sheep accident' and nevermore came to visit Lucia. Lucia begged her mother to explain what a 'sheep accident' was but her mother shook her head, pressed her lips together and would say no more. This, of course, grew large in Lucia's imagination. She knew her uncle had been a shepherd and she missed him— his fantastic lore mixed with elemental truths.

After that, Lucia took to squinting at the Matterhorn forlornly and searching for a human figure up there—one with a round belly. She comforted herself by imagining that Bruno lived at the top of the mountain with the cloud and candle fire and was waiting there for her, to celebrate her birthday one last time.

Life went on, although less vibrant without her beloved uncle. She started school—a girl with two tidy braids at a wooden desk, looking out the window. Water vapor and wind-she learned that is what clouds are made of. Physics and chemistry and meteorology didn't make sense to Lucia. Clouds were made of fluffy cotton tied together with dreams. Uncle Bruno had told her that, and she stuck stubbornly to it. It kept him alive in her memory but earned her a failing grade in Earth Science.

He's up there, she thought. She would not betray his memory with physical properties and chemical formulas. He lived in cloud shine, and if she dissected that magic she would betray his memory and lose him.

A few years later the railroad was rebuilt and improved and the tourists came, and after them came the seasonal workers. The population doubled, tripled, until it became more of a small city than a town. Lucia ventured to the village less and less, preferring her own company and that of the goats. The old families kept to their own. She missed her uncle desperately, but she was almost glad he wasn't around to see what was becoming of his beloved Zermatt.

On her way to school she had to walk the gauntlet, passing the rowdy pubs and discos. The air stank from permanent smell of cheese from fondues which the tourists consumed en masse. Lucia was relieved at the end of the school day to retreat to the mountains, far from the ski slopes, where she knew every stone and pebble by heart.

During her final year the school was renovated to accommodate the influx of new students, mostly the children of the guest workers. They spoke Portuguese, which sounded alien to Lucia's ears. She was one of the last children of the mountain who spent a simple childhood under those high blue skies and was more adept on skis and snowshoes than her own feet. The last generation to work the rocky ground and coax juicy apricots out of it and enough grass to feed the cows. That was Lucia's world. She did not know anything of stocks and shares and didn't even trust banks but could feed her mother, herself, and anyone else who might need a hand in winter on blue-tinged milk and light green cabbage. She and her mother were the only ones who didn't winter in town. Lucia went to school by snowshoes, sled or ski.

After she graduated from high school she stayed in the cabin with her mother, trying to forget everything she had been taught in school. Their cabin was near the trail that led to the Matterhorn, and the tourists would march right through the fields, crushing the tiny flowers, grass and fluffy cotton-like plants under their climbing boots. Lucia's mother Hannelore got the idea to open a small restaurant for the hungry climbers on the way. Hannelore spruced up the large patio that Uncle Bruno had built and furnished it with a couple wooden tables and hard-backed chairs that he had hacked out of thick pieces of wood. Lucia had sewn fluffy cushions for these chairs. 'Restaurant' was too grand a word for their business—it was more of a small outdoor dining room where the mountain climbers travelling to and from the Matterhorn could stop for a tea, bread or coffee. Jam depending on what season it was. Sometimes fresh berries. Cheese. Whatever happened to be in the icebox.

They chose the name Restaurant Stern, German for 'star'. Lucia worked there as a waitress. The tourists didn't understand her, even if she spoke as slowly as she could. She tried to pick up a little English from them, but never had the courage to say more than 'Water, sir?'

Most of the clients were British. The British had an unhealthy fascination with the Alps, the Matterhorn in particular. Lucia would see them coming up the path with their ropes and picks, wearing rough-hewn shirts and rugged pants. She would hurry to throw the red checked tablecloth over the table and start getting out the glasses and brewing coffee. There was always a prepared pot waiting. Eventually she learned to greet the guests in English. She could tell them the price in English, which she usually made up on the spot. The British had no idea of what a Swiss franc was worth, and Lucia had no idea what the value of the meal was. She would wish them luck.

Sometimes the men did not come back. The mountain ate them. The next time she would see them would be their marked graves behind the church in town.

Usually the survivors did not stop at the Restaurant Stern on their return journey, but if they did they were not as animated as they had been on the way up the mountain. The jolly conversation had been stolen by the vertical cliffs, shallow footholds and heaping snowdrifts of the Matterhorn. The mountain had changed them.

Lucia first met young James when she was seventeen. He made her spill the coffee. He had a scruff of beard and hazel eyes. He tried to speak to her but she blushed. She did not understand him, so she just said the numbers she had learned. "One franc fifty, please. Two twenty-five."

He ate with his two older companions, stealing glances at Lucia. He made her aware of her dress brushing around her legs. Something warm and tickly prickled in the center of her. She was trying both to avoid his gaze and at the same time attract it. She had never felt such mixed desires before.

The party finished their meal and marched off into the crisp morning, their path lit by the sun towards the mountain, his boots hidden under the grasses and tiny flowers of the alpine meadows. Lucia watched him go. He looked back and the sun was perched on his shoulder. He gave her a smile that rivaled the glare of the sun.

Lucia resolved to better her English. She found some ancient textbooks in the town's used book store (that was the only book store there was, new books were too expensive to import) and some children's books in English, probably left behind in one of the hotels by the children of British tourists. There was a story about a duck (a duck! Lucia marveled. She had never seen one) and a dog who seemed to get in a lot of trouble.

After her chores were done, Lucia would study before supper. At first it was impossible, familiar symbols arranged in strange combinations. Then she began to make connections: I ... that must be 'ich'. 'And' ... .that looks a lot like 'und'.

Lucia waited. As Spring turned to Summer her gaze wandered in the direction of Zermatt. Not that she could see the town directly. All visitors came up on a path that curved around the mountain. When she was working outside her attention always drifted that way, without her consciously being aware of it.

And she was not disappointed. One day in June James rounded the curve with the same two gentlemen who had been his companions last year. Lucia met his gaze and they both froze. Lucia's grin spread across her face like butter on warm toast and she hurried to prepare their table, her heart flying.

"Hello, how do you do?" She gave them a little bow.

"Very well, thank you," answered one of the older gentlemen. "And yourself?"

"Also well." Lucia smiled. "Today we have scones

with cream and jam. My mother make the jam and I make the cream with milk from our cows. I also make butter. I may bring you some?"

"Yes, please," the gentleman said.

James smiled at her. "You learned English?"

"A little." Lucia blushed.

"You are doing very well. Perhaps you can teach me German?"

"Maybe."

"Last year you only spoke in numbers."

"That the only English I knew."

"Three francs, two rappen, then." James winked at her.

"Two million two thousand!" Lucia exclaimed and scurried to get their meal.

When they were finished eating Lucia watched the crumbs that gathered at the corner of James' lips with something like endearment. He grinned at her through a mouthful of scone. As they got up to leave, Lucia gathered her cloak of courage around her. "You coming back next year?"

James looked down at her and grinned. "We do this every year, my father, my uncle and I. It's a tradition."

"I wait for you." Lucia promised.

That autumn was magic. Lucia sang more than usual as the ancient sun shone copper-slanted on the rocks and cliff and the air turned colder and crisper. Frost began to greet her in the morning. She saw her breath in front of her eyes as she milked the cows. The memory of James kept her warm in the icy depths of winter. She daydreamed of seeing him again through the long spring, as the flowers tentatively opened to the sun, gaining in strength and height.

Her whole world had narrowed down to June.

She had almost given up for the morning on June fifteenth when he appeared with his family. The sky was stone grey, but Lucia beamed enough to light up the mountain as she shook out the tablecloth with a great flourish.

"Today we have summer soup and biscuits."

"Thank you Miss Two million," James said.

He kept catching her gaze as she bustled around the patio and tipping his head. What could he possibly mean?

I want you to follow me.

He excused himself from the table and Lucia snuck around to the back of the house. There James was waiting. She opened her mouth to speak but he put a finger to her lips and then kissed her. Lucia's feet felt like they were leaving the ground. Everything inside her rose to meet him. She had never kissed anyone on the mouth before. She felt the mountain at her back, pressing her towards him.

"Your eyes are open," he said and laughed.

"I want to see you," Lucia answered.

When she kissed him, she tasted the ocean—a place she had never been before. Cliffs and beach and the rest of the world, highways and harbors and an endless sky. She felt something hard press against her inner thigh and desire blotted out the restaurant and the mountain and even Lucia herself. She had only one yearning, to take him inside her where she could see all he had seen, become all that he was. She looked into his hazel eyes and smelled his scent of earth and sea.

He moaned and moved the thin cloth of her panties to the side. The feel of his fingers between her legs tweaked her longing up a notch, although she hadn't believed it possible. She yelped as he entered her and it felt as though they were perfectly made for each other. He thrust into her, the delicious friction pumping her joy upwards. It was all narrowed down to this point. She surrendered and closed her eyes. She felt as though her fingertips could graze the wall of the universe, it was only him and her alone.

"Open your eyes again," he whispered in her ear.

She did and she was looking into his hazel pools of sunlight.

"I love you. Miss Three pounds fifty. I want to marry you."

But James never came back.

"Mami, I think it's time."

Lucia staggered into the house holding her back, which had given her trouble all through the pregnancy but now throbbing with ache. She clutched the doorframe in her other hand. She had been milking cows all morning (albeit much more slowly than she usually did) trying to shrug off the pain but her hands had become stiff and her concentration poor.

Hannelore leapt up from the table where she had been sewing, almost knocking it over. She steadied the table and hurried to Lucia's side, taking her elbow and leading her gently to the bedroom.

Lucia let out a breath between pressed lips as she perched like an awkward bird on the bed. „You can get the milk pail too. I couldn't finish milking Gerta but I got half a pail full anyway."

"Never mind the milk. You stay right here and I will fetch some towels and some scissors. Don't move. I'll be right back."

"I'm not going anywhere," Lucia promised. Scissors, she thought ominously. Why scissors?

After Hannelore left Lucia was overcome by an overwhelming compulsion to curl up in bed. She was wearing layer after layer of farm clothes, heavy denim material, cotton, things she had knitted and her Mom had knitted for her and her grandmother before that. They hadn't been able to afford bigger clothing so Lucia had just draped everything looser to make room for her growing belly. Now she began unpeeling herself as another cramp hit her. Oh no my sheets, she thought, I have to tell Mami to lay a few towels down on her bed to protect them. She had seen Gerta's birth a couple of years ago and remembered the mess it made. Better safe than sorry. Then she collapsed on the bed and stared at the ceiling breathing through her teeth until her mother arrived.

„How are you darling?" Her mother was floating above her, mopping her damp forehead with a wet cloth, like she did when Lucia had fever as a child.

"It hurts, I feel funny. And it's like the pain is coming from outside myself." She tensed as another

204

cramp hit her, wet and bloody. "I'm not going to survive this, am I?"

"Of course you will. Don't try to fight it, sweetheart. Just let it come."

Another contraction ripped through her and she gasped, clutching the mound of her stomach, which rolled with a will of its own. The pain wiped all thought away and she screamed as it seized her. Then the pain released her—like an animal, shaking her in its teeth and then letting her go. Teasing her, playing with her. Letting her think she might live through this before pulling her back into the spiraling cycle of agony.

"The pauses are there so you have the opportunity to rest for the next contraction," Hannelore said.

Lucia lay boneless on the bed, dwarfed by her huge mound of stomach. She didn't even have the energy to open her eyes.

"Open your eyes," James had said. "Look at me."

She forced them open and her mother was there, looking distressed. "Where is he, Mami? What did he do to me? Why am I all alone?"

Hannelore shook her head. She blotted at Lucia's forehead. "I am with you. We will make it through this."

"It's coming again," Lucia moaned. The pain was building up, she felt it inside her, outside her. It took over her body and twisted and tortured it.

"Push now!" Her mother's voice was far away. Lucia squeezed her eyes tight and screamed. She felt something huge leave her body and her scream faded out as she fell back on the bed. She gave up and let unconsciousness swallow her, and her last thought was of James: his hazel eyes, his blinding smile. Will my baby look like him? Will he be a boy? Or she a girl?

As she came back to consciousness she saw her mother scrubbing blood off the wall. It had been even messier than Gerta.

She had to strain to speak—her voice a whisper in her own ears. "What happened, Mama?"

Her mother jumped and let out a small shriek at the question. The scrub brush dropped from her hand.

Lucia leaned over to check the cradle placed by her bed.

Empty.

"Mama, where's my baby?"

"Lucia, oh, dear, sweet, Lucia." She scurried to Lucia's side and Lucia thought that her mother looked so young and so old at the same time—like an eighty-year-old woman in a thirty-five year old body.

"Mama, where's my baby?"

Her mother sat on the edge of her bed and took Lucia's hand. "I'm so sorry Lucia—"

"Don't say it!" Lucia yanked her hand away and clamped her hands over her ears. "I don't want to hear it!"

"Lucia." Her mother sternly took her hands away from her ears. "He died. A little boy. Your baby died. He didn't make it."

Lucia put her hands back over her ears and shook her head as grief erupted. Hot tears raced down her cheeks. Hannelore sobbed and tried to take Lucia into her arms. Lucia was as rigid as a fencepost, with tremors running through her. Her mother stroked her hair. "He's with Uncle Bruno now, my darling. He will be well taken care of."

Lucia shoved her mother and stood up but her legs wouldn't support her, she clutched on to a wooden chair.

"Where is he?" she demanded.

"I put his body on the table." Hannelore's chin quivered. "Lucia, we must bury him. We will wait until you are stronger, and then we will do it together."

"No!" Lucia roared. "We are not going to bury my baby! It's too dark, he'll be cold—"She let go of the chair and crumpled to the floor, but she dragged herself towards the table using only her arms.

"Lucia stop it!" Hannelore sobbed behind her. She half expected her mother to yank her back into bed but no hand fell upon her shoulder. She pulled herself determinedly forward.

From the floor she could see a bundle of blanket on the table. She hauled herself up, screaming with pain she did not feel. One hand held on to the chair and with the other she peeled the blanket back.

"You shouldn't cover his face," she chided her mother.

Hannelore wailed behind her. "Lucia—"

He was perfectly formed, lying on her mother's abandoned sewing. She gently opened one of his eyes, but it had rolled up, showing only white.

She couldn't tell if it was hazel.

She dressed her baby in the jumper she had knitted

for him— yellow to take care of every eventual possibility, girl or boy. Yellow like the sun. She marveled at his limp arms and legs. All the perfectly formed fingers, the perfect toes. He did not protest as she dressed him, but it was like trying to thread a needle as the thread weaved away from the hole. She moaned softly as she stuffed the little lifeless arm into the sleeve.

He had wispy blonde hair, like James. Lucia stroked his head, cooed and whispered a cracked lullaby to him, holding him close. She tucked his arms together over his stomach. He did not move. Tears slid down in sheets as she lay him back on the table. She had to clutch the chair again as she turned to her mother. She started to make her way back to Hannelore, holding herself upright with the wall.

Hannelore was standing in the doorway, her face tremendous wrinkled and red, clutching a towel— trying to dry her face and dam the flow of tears.

"Mami I—"

Lucia fainted, and knew no more.

Chapter 13

Cleona eyed the meteorite warily as it perched on her desk. She had scooped it up with her jacket after the paramedics left and carried it to her room for safekeeping. She was sure that no one noticed her during the ruckus, but she didn't know why she felt that she had to sneak it out. After all, Lucia had meant for her to have it. But she wasn't sure anymore if she wanted it. If Cleona believed in magic, she might have thought the meteorite to be cursed. It had brought Lucia bad luck. "Tell me all your secrets," she whispered to it, but from a safe distance, outside of what she thought to be the bad juju radiation zone. She was startled by her reflection in the mirror. "Don't be ridiculous," she told her alternate self. "There is no such thing as magic."

Sleep seemed impossible but she climbed into bed and turned off the light anyway. The meteor glittered, collecting the bit of moonlight in the room and reflecting it back by a factor that seemed impossible. The rock was aflame with silver moonlight. Cleo wasn't going to get too close to it, but she wasn't about to let this thing get more than a couple meters away from her until what? Until she could get it back to the lab? Until it was placed in a museum? Until her sponsor decided to use it as a doorstop?

She did not know what the future held for her treasure. But more important was what it was going to tell her about the past.

She sighed and threw off the covers. The meteor certainly wasn't cursed, she told herself as she approached it. There are no such things as curses. She stood over it, rubbing it gently with her thumb. It was lumpy and smooth. She could have sworn she felt a pull, as if she were capable of feeling magnetic force. She was contaminating the hell out of it, but she didn't care. Cleona closed her eyes and suddenly memories gushed forth, nuggets that had gotten buried like an Antarctic meteor under snow, but things she had never forgotten.

The meteor made Lucia forget, the meteor made Cleona remember.

She was swinging in her backyard, her blue Converse sneakers pointing towards the sky. An American childhood with Big Wheels and macaroni and cheese. She grew up in a small town in California, but Cleona had always been looking in another direction. Cleona saw herself at eight years old, climbing up the hill in her backyard, looking sometimes east towards Pennsylvania, sometimes up to the heavens, searching for meteors, sometimes west towards Vietnam. There was another childhood behind that childhood. Cleona knew it then, and she knew it now.

She spent a lot of time alone. She couldn't connect with her classmates. Unicorn lunchboxes and rainbow shoelaces held no deeper meaning for her.

One evening in winter she saw a ball of light streaking overhead. She gushed back inside the house, tracking a path of dirt behind her, and jumped up on the bar stool next to her mother who was slicing a carrot.

"Mommy (—but she wasn't your mommy was she? not really—) you can wish on shooting stars, can't you?"

"No Cleona. Those aren't really stars at all. They are rocks from outer space. You might as well make a wish on a brick wall."

"Rocks from space," Cleo repeated. She hung her head and traced the tile pattern on the counter forlornly with her finger. She had had her wish already picked out—she had wanted to hug her mother again. Not the lady in front of her, cutting vegetables, telling her that there were no such things as shooting stars and wishes. No, her real mother.

I was looking for my mother all along, Cleo thought. I just never knew in which direction to look.

Something howled overhead. Was she in her hotel room in Zermatt? Another meteor? Instead of touching carpet, her naked feet touched dirt—hard-packed under her toes and the ball of her heel. She gingered her way forward in the darkness cut by fire overhead but she had to be careful, the ground was rocky in places. She stepped on a sharp stone and she bent as if shot and cried out, pinwheeling her arms to keep from stumbling as pain raced up her leg. But she wasn't heavy enough that the rocks broke the skin. She was lighter, her feet were smaller. The stones flickered orange and red, the city was burning. Her whole world was burning.

This wasn't Zermatt. This wasn't California.

Then someone took her hand. She looked up. She had become so short! There was a woman towering over her, the sky on fire behind her. It was her mother with terrified eyes, shouting something into her face she didn't understand. Her mother was speaking Vietnamese. She started dragging Cleo, stumbling through the streets. Her mother kept glancing behind them, those black eyes brimming with worry.

Things were roaring overhead. Airplanes, helicopters, missiles, meteors? They had to clamor over debris in the street.

"Where are we going?" Cleona cried. In Vietnamese. She could speak in Vietnamese.

She heard the roar of airplanes overhead. Burning rocks were shooting down from the sky. Some buildings had been hit, crumbling into the filthy street. Little fires burned here and there. The muck mixed with something horrible- squashed between her bare toes as she ran through the street with her mother. For some reason there was clothing in the street, empty boots and torn shirts and trousers. Cleona clutched her mother's hand tighter.

It was 1975, and Saigon was falling.

Her mother, Cleona remembered her name was Nga Tran, yanked her through the streets as Cleona tried to keep up. The air stank of sulfur and ashes, with a darker underlying stench of burning hair. People were running in all directions, some shouting, some crying, some on fire. Tiny orange motes were drifting on the smoke currents and Cleona realized that even the dust was on fire.

"Hurry hurry!" Her mother yanked her arm hard.

The Americans were evacuating. The helicopters were perched on the roof of what had been Saigon's finest hotel. The pool area was filled with people, some standing on the lounge chairs. There was so much pushing and shoving that people were getting knocked into the pool. Nga Tran pushed her daughter forward through the throng of people crying "She white! She white!" She lifted Cleona and Cleona's nightgown rode up, she felt her mother's hands on the skin of her hips. "She American!"

An American soldier on the roof spotted them. He was assisting people into one of the helicopters. It was Cleona's eyes that proved the hypothesis—eyes as blue as ice, glittering terrified in the flickers of the burning city. He reached down and grabbed Cleona by her elbow and yanked her out of her mother's grasp onto the roof. "What's her name?"

"Cleona!" Nga shouted over the din of helicopters.

Cleona. Named after a tiny Pennsylvania town, a town Nga had found on a crumbling map of America. Cleona's father had mentioned that he came from Pennsylvania, a place in America. This had captured Nga's imagination, and she often wistfully looked at the map, her finger tracing roads she would never travel on.

Cleona's father. A soldier in Vietnam. From Pennsylvania.

"Mommy!" Cleona cried as the soldier shoved her

into the helicopter. Nga reached out her hand, but there was a commotion at the back of the crowd and Nga's waving arm disappeared in an ocean of people. Cleona searched frantically but Nga was gone. "Mama!" Cleona said, but her voice wasn't a little girl's voice. It was an adult woman's voice. Cleona looked down at her hands—her fingers were long, a woman's.

The helicopter lifted into the air. Cleona caught sight of her mother's upturned face. She wretched free of the soldier's grip and jumped three meters to the ground. Her mother smiled and held out her arms as Cleona leapt from the roof and stumbled into them. They clutched each other.

"Thank you Mom! Thank you for everything. You saved my life." She said it in Vietnamese, sobbing on her mother's shoulder.

Nga Tran smiled and pressed something into Cleona's hand. "You finally got your wish. Now go find your father."

Cleona opened her fist. Nga had put a crystal in it. An exquisite half of a mountain crystal.

When Cleona awoke in the bedroom in the hotel room in Zermatt, she was still clutching that piece of crystal. A shard of a dream. And maybe a wish about to come true.

Chapter 14

What a crazy ass night, Zachary thought as he lay in his bed. The green light of the smoke detector kept the darkness from being complete. And he had experienced more than his share of crazy ass nights. He was indeed the Captain of Crazy Ass Nights. He closed his eyes and the image of Lucia's limp body lying on the lobby floor floated behind his eyelids. He forced himself to shove that picture away—he had learned the art of turning off though all of his crazy ass nights. How to shut down his emotions while his mother paced the kitchen winding hers up. How to block out angry faces, desperate faces, frustrated faces. But then he thought of Emma's kiss. His skin still tingled where her lips had grazed him. He smiled as he drifted away.

He was surprised to find himself back at Anson's house, but he accepted the logic of dreams. They were in Anson's glassed-in porch, what his Mom called a winter garden, binge watching Zombie Cheerleaders. A ripped bag of potato chips was spilling crumbs on the end table but there were none ground into the carpet. An open bottle of soda threatened to foam over but no stains on the wood table. It was as though Anson's house was always clean with a layer of teenager smeared over it—so Zach guessed someone must be responsible for cleaning. And it certainly wasn't Anson—he barely remembered to shower after Phys Ed.

But Zach had never seen Anson's parents, not even once, and he had spent a lot of time hanging out at Anson's house. He supposed that Anson was his best friend, but he still didn't know much about his private life.

Zach was keeping his gaze locked straight ahead on the TV screen so he wouldn't glance at his phone. He didn't want to know what time it was or if he had any messages. Thank Christ that this episode of Zombie Cheerleaders was almost over. Zach had two pages of algebra still to do, a physics test tomorrow and a football match the next evening. He was itching to get home.

The credits started to roll and Anson leaned over at him and grinned, his face lit up like a half moon in the flickering light from the television. "One more?"

"No, man, I gotta go." Zach heaved himself out of the cushy blue chair that was threatening to devour him. How could a chair be so soft and comfortable?

"Oh come on ... .I gotta see what happens next! Don't you wanna know if Edward gets eaten and Carly can figure a way to get out of the locker? The suspense is killing me!" Anson put his hands around his throat and made gagging noises.

"Seriously, I gotta go. It's already—"Zach allowed himself a peak at his phone. There was a missed telephone call from his mother. Shit. "Almost ten. I was supposed to be home at 9:30."

"Pussy. Well can you at least take me to the 7-11? I have a life-threatening Twinkie deficiency in my blood."

"Sorry dude, I'm here with my bike."

"We can take my Dad's car."

Zach wondered again where Anson's parents were. "I don't have my license."

"You have your permit, don't you? Come on. Drive me there and back. Five minutes. I gotta have me my Twinkies!" Anson started jumping around on the blue chair and took a swig of cola, letting it dribble over his lips like he had rabies.

Why don't you drive? Zach wanted to ask. Why don't you walk? But it was easier to say yes to Anson than to argue with him. Zach liked Anson, he was fun to be around, but Anson had the annoying trait of not being able to say goodbye well. He always wanted to draw every hangout session out to its bitter end. It was easier for Zach to just play along and not argue with him.

"C'mon!" Anson sprang off the chair and bounded through the garage door. He flicked on a light and Zach gasped when a blue Corvette was illuminated. Convertible, top down.

"Aw man. I'm not sure about this—"

"Hop in, dude. My dad won't give two fucks in a chicken stall."

In spite of his nervousness, Zach laughed. "Two fucks in a chicken stall, where did you get that one?"

"Or two balls in a tennis match." Anson winked and jumped in the passenger side without even opening the door. "Let's roll, dude."

Zach opened the driver's side and fell into the car. The Corvette was built low to the ground. A stick shift jutted towards Zach. He stared back at it. His Driver's Ed teacher had one of those, but he had practiced more on his mother's car, which was an automatic.

Anson tossed him the keys.

"Where's the start button?" Zach searched by the steering wheel.

Anson pointed to a hole for the ignition. "Dude this is an oldie. That's why I gave you the keys. You need to do this manually."

"Oh." Zachary had never done that before, but seen it in movies. He inserted the key and turned. Nothing.

"It doesn't work." He tried to coat the relief in his voice with disappointment. "Looks like no Twinkies for you today dude."

"You Dumbbot. You have to push the clutch and the brake in."

"Oh." Anson wasn't worried that he couldn't start the car. Worry was not in Anson's emotional repertoire. Zach did as he was told and turned the key again. The Corvette's engine purred to life. He let the clutch go and the car jolted forward.

"Reverse buddy, you have to put it in reverse. You have to push the stick down while you shift."

"How do I know if I'm in reverse?"

Anson laughed. "You'll go backward."

Zach did it again and this time the car lurched backward. "Fast learner," Anson joked. "Let's go!"

Zach started to ease out of the garage. The car jolted and stalled as he hit the garage door. "Oh shit."

"My bad." Anson pressed a button attached to the rear view mirror. "I forgot to open the door."

The garage door rattled open and Zach babied the Corvette out of the garage, praying that there was no mark on either the door or the bumper.

Night had settled while they had been watching Zombie Cheerleaders. Zach didn't even want to know how late it was. It would stress him even more. He already felt like a guitar string tuned too tight. He tried to turn on the headlights and turned on the blinker instead. Anson laughed.

The range of vision was much closer to the ground than Zach was used to. He scraped the undercarriage of the car over the speed bump used to mark the end of Anson's housing development. The Corvette shuddered and buckled through the late twilight under the glow of the streetlights. Anson was swinging his arm like a cowboy with a lasso and making a 'whoop whoop' sort of noise. Zach was trying to keep his attention focused on the road.

They almost made it. They were two and a half blocks away from 7-11 when it happened.

Zach never even saw the woman until she was splattered across the Corvette's hood. She seemed to come from nowhere, almost as if she had fallen from the sky. Then she rolled off the side of the car and there was a sickening thud as the car ran her over. Anson's whoop-whoop cut off immediately. The Corvette bucked and stalled.

"Ah, fuck, man! Did you hit her?" Anson's voice bordered on hysteria, as high as a woman's.

Zach glanced over at Anson. His eyes felt loose in his sockets and his stomach was filled with mossy rocks. "I—I think so." He heaved himself out of the car and threw up.

*

"I can't afford that," Amanda said. She was pacing back and forth in her tiny kitchen while she spoke to her ex-husband—quick to the stove, a peek in the refrigerator, tracing the dial on the oven. She was never able to sit still when she spoke to him.

"Look," Steve said. "This is a make-or-break moment. If we do the wrong thing here Zach's future will be ruined. He'll never go to college or get a job or get married or start a family. Is that what you want?"

"Of course not. But that lawyer you found is just too expensive. There's no way I can pay half. $5,000 for a retainer is just ridiculous! Who knows how much this is going to end up costing us!" She forced herself to lower her voice. Zach's bedroom door was closed but she never knew how much he could hear. She had already met Bill Silverman, the lawyer, across the table at the divorce hearing. His hand had scraped hers when she shook it, like sandpaper. The idea that she had to pay him anything, even for Zach's sake, made her furious.

"Look," Steve said again. Amanda clenched her jaw. He was always trying to get her to 'look', to perceive things the way he saw them, to cross over to his point of view. It had been that way during their marriage. There was no reason why it should be any different after their marriage was over. When it had been her turn to speak in discussions he was watching NFL on television or hid his face behind a newspaper or scrolled on his tablet. Amanda wondered fleetingly if he listened to his new wife, Bethany, who was 20 years younger than she was, more attentively than he had listened to her.

"Bill Silverman is the best. There's no one better than him. He says that the woman Zach hit had a heart condition anyway, and was also mentally unstable. She was homeless when Zach ran her over and her blood alcohol level was 1.3. Silverman thinks that we might even be able to avoid a manslaughter charge for Zach. That means nothing goes on his record and he can move on with his life and we all can forget this ever happened. Isn't that what you want as well?"

"Steve. For the third time now, I can't afford it. What I want is a moot point. I don't know what language I have to say it in that you understand. Bill Silverman may be the best, I don't doubt it." He sure did all right for you, she thought. "But he is way out of my price range."

"Well, I'm not footing this bill alone. Our divorce decree says we split all expenses for Zach straight down the middle. And I'm still paying alimony and child support so I'm already paying more than half."

"Steve, I'm on a tight budget as it is! The amount that you pay me isn't enough for a cockroach to live on. I don't think I can make rent this month— child support, alimony or not. I'm probably going to have to ask the landlord for another extension! There's no way I can pay anyone, even John Dillinger, a $5,000 retainer."

"I would think about that if I were you." Steve's voice was tight and Amanda remembered the way his thin lips disappeared when he was angry. She wasn't free of him, even after the divorce. "I would think about it hard. I would take out a loan if I were you. Pawn your jewelry. It's our son's future we are talking about!"

"I understand that, Steve. Probably even better than you do. But it's too expensive. I'm sorry but I just won't be able to pay half. Period."

"Look. As far as I'm concerned this happened on your watch." And with that bomb he had her. As soon as he accused her of anything, whether subtle or direct, her stomach plummeted and her defenses shot up. It had been like that since they had gotten engaged. "You were the one who allowed him to go see this Anson kid. You are the one responsible for raising him. He spends most of his time with you."

"Why would I have forbidden him from visiting his friend? How was I supposed to know he would get in a car and hit a pedestrian? It isn't my choice to be a single parent, by the way! That's all on you."

Steve sighed and the telephone line ached with it. "I am tired of cleaning up your messes, Amanda. I have arranged that our son doesn't have to pay eternally for your screw-ups and all you have to take responsibility for your mistake by footing half the bill. Only half, mind you! How you do it is your problem. Maybe you need a second job."

"You mean a third."

"Whatever. It's your problem. You can send the check to Bill Silverman. $2,500 by Wednesday or we lose him." Steve hung up.

Amanda stared at her cell phone as if it had personally offended her, beating down the urge to throw it across the room. If it broke it was just another thing that she couldn't afford to replace.

The kitchen in her new apartment wasn't a bad place, it had been compact and tidy when she first moved in. Of course it didn't compare to the lavish kitchen with marble countertops that she had in the old house she had shared with Steve. But her current apartment was more or less hygenic and it wasn't actively neglected. Amanda just lacked the time and energy and financial resources to make it House Beautiful.

She kept pacing her kitchen. She could do it in three giant steps. Pawn your jewelry, Steve had said. She didn't want him to know that she had already done that. For the electric bill last December. And she had gotten much less than it was worth. There was no way she was going to come up with $2,500 by Wednesday. She didn't have anything left worth that much.

Not even my body, she thought. I couldn't even sell that.

Then she remembered the meteorite.

Her grandfather had discovered it in a field he had been plowing, and he had kept it on a sideboard in the dining room. As a child Amanda had been fascinated by it, sticking paper clips to it because it was magnetic. Her grandfather had willed it over to her when he died.

It might be worth something, Amanda thought.

She hurried down the hall, but stopped cold in front of Zach's door. We need a break when this blows over, she thought as she stroked the wood. If we could only get out of here for a while, I'm sure things would look better. Amanda hadn't had a vacation since the divorce, it was long overdue. She rushed into her bedroom. She had to take all her winter sweaters down to get to the meteorite's box, hidden all the way in the back. It was about as big as a football and heavy, made of iron and nickel.

She carried it to the dining room table which doubled as her desk and opened up her three-year-old laptop. It took a while to power up. It would need to be replaced soon, but just now she couldn't afford it. She stuck a few paperclips to the meteorite for old time's sake while she waited for her laptop and started composing the Craig's list ad in her head.

Chapter 15

She wasn't sure which blood was the old woman's and which was her own, but her white gown was splattered with it. It glowed bluish in the night. Astra halted, held onto a fence post and tried to catch her breath. Where should she go? The ice goddess in her was fleeing and she felt cold creeping in—it felt like freezing needles stabbing in her pores. So this is what being cold feels like, she thought. I never knew. She closed her eyes and an image of her frozen, open-mouthed corpse floated into her vision. She saw her dead body perfectly, snowflakes falling from a clear sky into her eyes as she looked up sightlessly at the stars.

She pushed the image away. She had to decide where to go. If she went back to the Flock of Flakes the police would find her as sure as a mountain goat finds grass. And now through her own impulsive craziness there was an entire herd of witnesses to her attack on Lucia. She had not only dug her own grave, she had already sent out invitations to her own funeral.

She looked up to the mountains; they were glowing in the night like the blood on her gown. They looked like sentinels, no longer welcoming. They were the same mountains that had killed her parents, not the mountains which protected her. Whatever superpowers Astra had possessed had been revoked with interest.

But beyond their steep sharp peaks lay Italy, a place she had heard legends of but never seen. Maybe she could get Rufus, grab a few supplies and escape to Italy.

In the end she had no choice. She had to go back at least to change out of her bloody clothes and scavenge some of the donations to finance her escape. She had to sneak back into camp.

She skirted the pools of streetlight. Only shadows passed her on the streets but she still felt conspicuous in her red-spattered white frock. She heaved a sigh of relief when she passed the last house on the outskirts of the village without being seen by the living and mounted the trail back into the mountains.

There was a tricky part on the way to Lucia's cabin, where the path narrowed. A place where hikers had to move single file lest risking tumbling over the edge. It was even more hazardous with the snow. She stopped short as she rounded the corner. A dark figure was hulking over the trail on the narrowest part of the path. Was it a policeman? Were they looking for her already? But the figure stood motionless as she approached, making no move to arrest her.

"Who are you?" Astra called out. "I am the High Priestess of Winter. I advise you to make way."

"There used to be wolves in these mountains." She couldn't see his face, but his voice was deep and gravelly, as if he had swallowed stones from the bottom of a grave, stones which had never seen the light.

"Look, I don't want any trouble. I just want to get back to my camp. If you would kindly move to the side, that I may pass. The trail is narrow here."

"If you want to pass, priestess, then you must pass through me."

In spite being scared, cold and miserable, Astra laughed. "I may be thin, but there's no way I can get around you."

The dark figure moved, perhaps he was shrugging. "I'm not moving. Your choice. Go back down this mountain and confess your crimes. Or try to get by me. Your choice."

"My crimes?"

"Yes. Or did you butcher a sheep? Like the wolf?"

Astra considered. This was the only trail up the mountain in winter. And she wasn't going back down.

"No it wasn't a sheep." She kept her voice soft and deadly. "It was a person. And if you don't want to be next you had better make way."

No word from the figure, but he moved a bit off the trail towards the mountain side. "Wise choice." Astra said. As approached him she smelled frozen death that was beginning to thaw, but it was too late to go back. Keeping her eyes fixed straight ahead she moved to pass him but a tremendous shove pushed off her feet. She slipped off the path and from the cliff. For a moment she felt like she was flying. She landed in a snowbank and there was a snap that she felt as well as heard as multiple bones in her body broke. Freezing snow filled her mouth and nose and she couldn't breathe.

The man above her nodded. A gust of wind lifted surface snowflakes in the air and the figure disappeared in the cloud. He left no footprints. Astra would be found in the Spring thaw, mouth open, sightless eyes staring into the sky.

Sunlight illuminated the dining room at Hotel Bergkrystall, and cheerful morning rainbows danced in every corner. Cleona found Reginald there, eating oatmeal and examining a newspaper. He appeared to be observing it rather than reading it, his eyebrows wrinkled and pulled together, his thoughts perhaps elsewhere. He noticed her and put it aside. The rustling of the newspaper and Vera chewing her toast and slurping her orange juice were the only noises in the dining room. The other guests had gone skiing or shopping or whatever it was normal people did on holiday. "Miss Skye, good morning. You look as though you didn't sleep very well."

"Doctor Skye." Cleona sat down across from him. "No, I didn't sleep well. Restless sleep tends to accompany eventful days, as the human brain tries to process the incidents of the day. I suppose I had a lot to process. I had very odd dreams."

"Sorry to hear." He laid his newspaper aside. "Are you enjoying your meteorite?"

"I'm not certain yet. It's strange. I wanted it so much that it made me forget about what is right, and what is wrong. I suppose that I behaved as badly as young Mr. Zach. Now I possess it, I still must discern how I feel. It seems almost anti-climatic." She cleared her throat. "How is Lucia?"

"I called the hospital first thing this morning. The nurse said she was stable, but didn't want to put me through to her room because she was sleeping. I plan to visit her as soon as I finish my breakfast."

"Where's her dog?"

"Sparky's enjoying his time in the lobby with Emma's dog, Askia. I think they've formed quite a friendship." Reginald wiped his lips with the pristine cloth napkin. "Would you like some coffee, Doctor Syke? I haven't seen Emma yet this morning but there's another waitress who seems perfectly capable of bringing you a cup. She brought me a fairly decent oatmeal. With cinnamon."

"I think after everything we've been though, you can call me Cleo."

"All right Cleo."

"My full name is Cleona."

"Ok then, Cleona."

"There is a town called Cleona in Pennsylvania."

"What a coincidence. I'm from Pennsylvania."

"My father was as well." Cleona leaned forward. "You know, Reginald, can I call you that? Reginald? I never met my father. Even my mother hardly knew him. They only spent one night together. But he had told her that he was from Pennsylvania. My mother never visited there, she never left Vietnam, but she had a map of the States. She saw the name 'Cleona' on that map, and so I was named after a place she had never been, in honor of a man I had never known."

"Until now." She reached into her pocket and put the crystal on the table.

"You took my crystal again?" Reginald raised one eyebrow. "How did you manage that? Are you planning on a career as a pickpocket if your geology plans fail? Or did you learn that from young master Zachary?"

"Check your pocket." Cleona rested one trembling finger on the spike of the crystal. "Just do it."

He did, and his eyes widened. With a shaky hand he put his crystal on the table, next to hers. Cleona put them together and they clicked into place.

A perfect match.

Cleona and Reginald stared at each other in the sunny dining room as rainbows danced on the walls. The light of the crystals was everywhere.

"I never used to believe in coincidence. But the odds of this are astronomical." Cleona's voice shook with the strain of trying to keep calm but the film of tears thickened over her eyes—her blue eyes. "My father gave this crystal to my mother. To thank her for saving his life, what he said she did."

"I had just lost a soldier," he said softly, with wonder. "I just needed some comfort. To touch someone, to be touched."

Cleona shook her head. She smiled ruefully and the tears were released. "I think you did a bit more than just touch each other, but I really don't need details. She gave me this crystal. It was the last thing she gave me before I was evacuated by the Americans. She told me that it belonged to my father."

"That it belonged to you."

They regarded each other across the table in a room filled with prismed light.

Chapter 16

Reginald strolled down the hospital hall, holding the lead awkwardly in his hand. He had never walked a dog before. He had to force himself to concentrate, the feel of the leash in his palm, his footfalls in the hallway, Sparky's playful yellow aura bouncing up and down as he walked. Cleona was still whirling in his head.

"Entschuldigung, sir?"

Reginald held his breath and turned around. Here it comes, he thought. They are going to ask me to leave with the dog.

But there was only a scrap of a man in a wheelchair, his aura a sick maroon. "Yes?" Reginald asked.

"Is your dog friendly? May I pet him?"

Reginald smiled. "Of course."

Sparky had enjoyed the taxi ride from Zermatt to Visp, where Lucia had been hospitalized. The dog had kept his head out of the window the entire way; Reginald figured that it had probably been his first trip in a car.

Sparky allowed himself to be cuddled, his friendly look never wavered. The man whispered something to the dog, nodded to Reginald and rolled on.

Room 402. This was it. He rapped on the door but there was no answer so he gentled it open and Sparky nudged his way inside. The walls were dirty yellow as if the room was trying to be cheerful despite absorbing decades of sorrows, and stank of disinfectant and urine. Lucia didn't turn around when they entered the room. He knew that she was awake, because he saw her open eyes reflected in the hospital window. The rest of her body was rolled under a hospital blanket, her grey hair loose and fanning over the pillow.

"Lucia?"

No reaction. The ghost Lucia in the window didn't even blink. Her sickly pale yellow aura shimmered weakly. Sparky barked with delight and bounded to the other side of the bed to lick Lucia's face. She didn't react. Sparky whined and sat in front of his mistress, tail slapping the floor hopefully.

"Lucia," he said again. "Are you all right? The nurse I talked to said the operation went well, and you can go home soon."

She didn't turn around.

"I have something to tell you," Reginald said. "Something incredible. And I could use your advice."

"Why I should care?" The lump on the bed answered. "Why I should help you?"

Sparky whined again.

"Well, I did help get rid of your investation problem. The Snowflakes are gone. When you are released from here you can go back home and your troubles will be over." Reginald reached out to touch her hair, but he pulled his hand back. "Lucia, what's wrong? Is there something the nurse didn't tell me?"

"Everything fine. Seventeen stitches."

"Is it Astra? Are you worried about her? The police are searching for her. I'm sure they will find her."

"Is not about crazy Snowflake." She shook her head into the pillow. "I give meteor to Cleona, I remember. I remember everything." She turned away from the window to stare at the ceiling. "I remember why I want to forget."

"Forget what, Miss Lucia?"

"I lose him now twice." Tears wandered down the wrinkle trenches of her cheek. "Twice. Once more than plenty." She rolled back to the window. "I want die now. I already dead. Just wait for broken heart stop beating."

"Who was it that you lost, Miss Lucia?"

"My son. My baby. I wish on falling star to forget him." More tears streamed down her cheek and pooled by her ear. "I live every day of life with death. Since he die. He never help milk cow, harvest, go school." She starting sobbing. "Go away, Reginald." She said between hitches. "I want be alone."

"Of course, because you haven't been alone enough in your life until now?" He touched her shoulder. "Miss Lucia, you aren't alone any longer. You don't need to carry this burden by yourself any more. I am here for you now, as well as all those other fools back at the hotel."

"You no understand." Her gaze was fixed on the ceiling. Her lower jaw trembled and the tears kept coming. "I know life without memory. This life much better. Make friends, laugh. Memory come back, take laughter. If I die, maybe I can be with son."

"What was your son's name?"

"Colin. His name Colin. You know, once I get sick,

after he die, I get fever. He visit me then, Colin. He had an entire life with harvests and school and marriage and children. Then I get better, and I remember that Colin is dead. Colin was never alive. I lose him again and again."

"Miss Lucia, look at me."

She turned slowly to Reginald, chest hitching. He reached out and stroked her wet cheek. Their gazes locked and Lucia let out a deep breath.

"Miss Lucia you are the guardian of memory."

"The what?"

"The guardian of memory. And that is never an easy job."

Her gaze locked onto him, clutched him like a drowning woman. In that moment Reginald realized that some part of her did want to live. It was up to him to give her a reason.

"You know what elephants are? They show elaborate grief rituals when another elephant dies. And sometimes their young are born dead. They cuddle the lifeless body and mourn. That is what you must do with the memory of your son. If you weren't alive anymore, there would be no one to remember Colin. It would be as if he never existed. You owe it to him. If you love him, you must keep his memory alive. You must remember."

"I only know him dead. I never hear him cry. I hold his dead body, like the elephant. But I never tell him story or kiss him goodnight or make him dinner."

"Then you owe it to the memory of what could have

been. Without you, he is lost. Every soul must have a candle burning for them on earth. Someone who remembers them. You are that for Colin."

"I never even know him!" she wailed. "How I supposed to honor his memory?"

"Because he mattered to you. Because you cared. You loved him for what he was, and also for what he could have been. He visited you in a dream. Therefore he is real."

She smiled ruefully. "You a funny man. I dreamed him, so he is real."

"Maybe you can communicate with him when you sleep. Maybe he left that door open." He took her hand and kissed it. "Love is holy, and it should never be in vain."

"Ha!" She snatched her hand back. "Why you so wise in heart matters? He who never love?"

"I did love! I did. I was going to get married, Lucia. And my fiancée died while I was away at war. And after I returned, I found out that she had been pregnant. I, too, know about loss. And so I am learning again how to love." He cupped her quivering chin in his hand. "And now you matter to me, dear Lucia. I will help you carry your burden."

She smiled weakly and swiped at her tears. "I never have help before. I know not how to take it."

"I'll teach you." He stroked her hair. "I am a beginner at this myself."

"Beginner at what?"

"At relationships. All I know is that I want to spend more time with you. It was you I was supposed to find. I knew it from the minute I saw your picture at the doctor's office."

Sparky licked her face and this time she smiled. She patted Reginald's hand. "You good man, colonel. What you want tell me? When you come in room?"

It didn't seem right after she had just shared her incredible loss to tell her about Cleona, but she was waiting for him to speak. So he gave her a summary of the morning's events with Cleona in the dining room.

"Wonderful!" Lucia exclaimed and as she struggled to sit up. "You have daughter."

"The thing is, Miss Lucia, I don't. My father visited Switzerland, but he never brought home a piece of mountain crystal as a souvenir. He never came back at all. His grave is in the Zermatt church cemetery."

She looked puzzled and absently stroked Sparky's fur. "I not understand."

"I got the crystal from someone else." He told her then about the death of Private Miller, omitting the condition of his body. "As he was dying, he told me: It is she who will find you. Then he pressed the crystal into my hand. Then he died."

"He make you guardian of his memory?"

Reginald grinned. "Perhaps."

"So you not Cleona's father?"

"No, I'm not. Private Miller was her father."

"You tell her?"

"It wouldn't be fair to her if I didn't."

Lucia smiled ruefully. "She don't want fair. She want father. Maybe you are guardian of his memory."

"I never dreamed—I never dreamed that I could have a child."

Lucia squeezed his hand. "I think Private Miller give you present. He say she find you, and she find you."

"Yes, he did indeed. I just thought he was talking about you."

"Maybe both." They regarded each other in the ugly hospital room. Sparky barked and wagged his tail.

Chapter 17

Reginald's eyes opened in the dark. Where was he? When? Not Vietnam. Not Pennsylvania.

Then consciousness caught up with him and he remembered. Of course he remembered. Remembering was what he did best. The lump next to him was Lucia. He had taken her home from the hospital. He was staying with her.

He lay back down and let thoughts spin in his head: a new daughter; fine, leather shoes empty of feet; a key dangling on a string; a loon's cry before dawn; fog on a pond. Something was about to happen. The naked winter air felt like a cold blade to his chest, and he felt energy in his body as if he were young again. The moon was full, and the light flooded the tiny bedroom, illuminating Sparky on his blanket in the corner. The silence was complete, except for Lucia's breathing. There were so many stories in her breaths, and now they told him that she was also awake. She touched his shoulder, and his skin warmed under her fingers. "It's time," she said.

"Time?" Reginald asked. For what? For coffee? For snow? For spring?

"For me to go."

"Go?"

"Yes. I go meet Uncle Bruno on mountain."

She had mentioned Uncle Bruno before, and he somehow understood that this leaving would be permanent. It was logical—if she had an uncle, he was most likely dead. She wasn't talking about dropping in at a relative's for tea.

He surveyed her in the moonlight. It lit up half her face, just like the picture in the magazine when he had first seen her. "What are you talking about, Lucia?"

She sat up, clutching the blanket around her. "In hospital, doctors find something by my heart. Like tumor. Getting bigger. Starving heart. They tell me I could die anytime."

He sat up as well. "What? Are you sure?"

"Yes. I sure."

"Why didn't you mention this before?"

She smiled in the darkness. "Am old now. Waste of time to count ways I could die."

"But we could all die at any time! Any one of us!" He pounded his leg with his fist. "There's no need to rush the process!"

"Yes but I have death sentence."

"We all have a death sentence! That's the one true thing about life—it's always deadly.

She took a deep shaky breath. "One hour ago I woke up with it. Heart is choking, like doctor say. I almost wake you, but then I wait. Pain go away. This time, pain go away. But next time? I no wait for death. I meet in on my feet."

"Are you sure?"

"Yes. I ready."

Reginald felt something odd, there was pressure in his eyes. "I don't want you to go." One rebellious tear, shining in the moonlight, even managed to escape. When was the last time Reginald had cried? He did a cursory memory search and for once, came up empty.

Lucia closed her hand over his. "Now is time for me. I feel death coming on my heart. I know I no longer have so much time."

"But I just found you." He sat up in bed. "Please don't leave me now."

The moonlight shone through the freshly repaired window and Lucia's eyes were filled with light. "When, then? When is a good time to leave you? In three weeks? A month? A year when I no anymore can walk and I don't anymore know my own name and you are so tired of caring for me but can't anymore let me go?"

"Well, yes." Reginald lifted his chin. "It may be selfish of me but don't I get to spend a little bit of time with you? I came all this way, helped you with your problems, and now I just want to enjoy you for a while, make you happy for a bit because you deserve it. Is that so wrong, Lucia? Isn't that what you want too?"

She looked at him and he drew a sharp breath. He could see in her eyes that she was already halfway to heaven. "What I want is you to walk there with me. I am ready but scared too."

Reginald looked away. "How can you do this to me? You of all people? You know exactly what it's like to lose someone, to have to always imagine the life you would be having with them, if circumstances were different."

She threw off her bedcovers. "No bad feelings. It is much to ask, I know. You take care of Sparky for me? If you can't, take him to animal doctor in town? They find a home for him. He good dog, good friend."

Hearing his name, Sparky's tail thumped on the ground.

"No, Spark. This time I go alone."

"Where exactly are you going?" Reginald demanded, trying to keep the petulance out of his voice.

"I meet death on my feet." Lucia said as she pulled on her socks. "I not lay in bed and wait for death find me."

"What are you planning to do? Jump off a mountain? Walk until you collapse? This is insane, Lucia. Come back to bed. Let's stay right here in this cabin with each other for as long as possible and enjoy whatever time we have together."

"No hide from death." Lucia pulled on her pants. "Death always find you. Time with you would be beautiful, I know. But always not enough. Always too short."

"But that's what all of life actually is!" Reginald roared. "An intermission! A postponement of death! What difference would a few weeks make? Why won't you do it for me?"

She touched his cheek tenderly. "In a few weeks we talk same, but harder to say good-bye. I woke up now ready, and this is what I do. No bad feelings, you don't come with me. Too much to ask. But you let me go, Reginald. While I still can. This last gift you give me."

She put on her layers of clothing and Spark wagged

his tail again, his brown eyes looking hopeful. "Thank you, Sparky." She stroked his furry head and a sob escaped her. The dog looked at her with mournful eyes and whimpered. He didn't move to join her, as if he understood.

"Please take him care," she said, not looking at Reginald. "I tell you now, I saw lawyer in Visp. Dog is now your dog, cabin is your cabin, everything in it yours."

"Lucia—"

"And Colin. His memory yours now too. Now you keep that alive. You tell Cleona. But no tell Cleona about soldier Miller. Tell Cleona about love. What people do out of love." Her eyes shone.

"What about Cleona and those other idiots back at the hotel? Don't you even want to say goodbye to them?"

"Reginald. Let me go. Please. I beg you now." She didn't turn around. "Strange, though. I never know it until now. The more you love, the more you sad. The more you love, the more it hurts."

He sunk back down into the bed. She shivered and opened the bedroom door, closing it again, not looking back.

He heard her put on her coat and boots, the chair scraping the floor. There was a minute of silence, in which he could imagine her looking around the cabin, saying goodbye to her home and belongings. Then the sound of the outer door squeaking open and then thudding closed. Sparky lumbered over to the bedroom door, laying his paw on it as if to say goodbye.

Reginald's tears burst forth. An old man's tears—selfish tears, he thought. She had lost a son, he had found a daughter. What kind of man was he, that he couldn't even fulfill her last request?

He sprung out of bed and ran outside in his boxer shorts and t-shirt. Sparky ran with him. He didn't even feel the cold. "Lucia? Lucia!"

He saw her ahead on the path, a dark form under a silver moon, the snow a sparkling blanket all around. "Reginald!" she called. "You let me go now!"

"No I am coming with you! Wait!"

He dashed back inside and pulled on his clothes as fast as he could. Sparky was bounding about like a puppy with his tongue a pink ribbon.

He hurried outside. She was still waiting. He rushed to her.

She was smiling like a newborn star. He could see how beautiful she had been, how beautiful she still was. "You change mind?"

He took her mittened hands in his. "I said that I wanted to spend as much time with you as possible, didn't I?"

"Yes you did." And it was her turn to cry. "But no stop me, Reginald."

"I won't. I promise. I'll just—accompany you for a bit."

They pushed out into the frozen night. It was as if the coldness of outer space had touched down on this one spot. Reginald was so numb he felt weightless.

"Stars so close. God so close." Reginald looked around and was overwhelmed with the gorgeousness. The gem-stars mounted on the velvet black night. How the snow seemed to glow from within. Lucia pointed toward the Matterhorn, a silent guardian of the landscape. "My Uncle Bruno tell me that the entrance to heaven two kilometers this way. I remember now. I go there."

"The entrance to heaven?"

"Yes. As little girl I think that Uncle Bruno is on Matterhorn after he die. I no anymore climb so far, this tunnel is short way."

"The Matterhorn is heaven?"

Lucia shook her head. "I not know this, but it point up."

They trudged on, sometimes through knee deep snow. Soon it would all melt and Spring would come to the mountainside. For the first time in many years, without Lucia. Reginald's head spun with a thousand thoughts. A thousand things he wanted to tell her—the time he stole a candy bar when he was five, how much he missed his parents, how hideous Vietnam had been. Please wait until the snow melts and the warm wind blows. Wait until the flowers come out. Until the sun warms the earth. The autumn leaves turn to gold. Christmas. Oh please wait Lucia.

She was right, he thought as they marched wordlessly on. Like war, like illness, there is never a good time for death. The best you can be is ready. Reginald took her mittened hand and Sparky kept pace beside them. Not bounding like a puppy, not downtrodden but nobly marching. It was the last thing they could do for Lucia, accompany her on her final walk, and

Sparky intended to do it right. The least Reginald could do was keep the pace, with all his unuttered thoughts eddying behind them.

Lucia kept her gaze fixed straight ahead. Her chin was trembling. Maybe the cold. Maybe fear. Reginald clutched her hand tighter.

She squeezed his hand in return. "What you think death is like, Reginald?"

New images flashed through Reginald's mind ... .Private Miller and all the soldiers he had seen die in Vietnam, with their limbs blown off, open mouths splashed in blood, eyes wide in horror. And then his own personal belief that nothing existed after death. One's heart stopped beating and brain stopped thinking and they knew no more.

"I never really thought about it," he answered.

"Liar." But she smiled gently. "Don't forget that death brought you here, and death give you daughter. Death give you reason to live."

"And you?"

"I finished now. This last great adventure." She looked at him and he saw the young girl that she had been in her eyes, as if time was now running backward for Lucia. "I never be out of valley before, Reginald. I never left the mountain. Trip to the hospital in Visp was most far away from home I ever go."

Stay with me, he thought. I will show you cities, deserts, jungles, oceans.

"You will do fine," he said.

She stopped abruptly. "There. Look."

He and Sparky halted too and he followed her finger with his gaze. On the side of the mountain was a cave surrounded by snow. It looked as though the aurora borealis shone out from inside the cave. Rainbow-colored light was streaming out and all the full moon-silvered snow reflected crystalline colors. Reginald gasped. There were even more rainbows than the dining room back at the hotel.

Lucia squeezed his hand. "The rest of way I go alone."

Reginald turned to her, cupped her chin in his hand. "Let me go with you."

"Soon I sure. But you just found daughter. Stay a bit with her. I meet you on other side from mountain."

"In Italy?" His voice cracked.

She smiled. "No, the other other side."

"What if I told you that I will remember you until I die?" he asked. "The first time you smiled at me, how bad your coffee tastes, your hand on the back of my neck. Everything, Lucia. Everything. I will keep your memory."

She took a step away from him and squeezed his hand one last time before dropping it. He reached out to snatch her hand back but forced himself to put it back firmly at his side. She turned to face him and he saw that she was crying. "This really hard."

The sky was getting lighter. "Please." He knew he shouldn't but he couldn't help it. He felt like a razor blade was spinning around and cutting him up inside. "Just watch one last sunrise with me. We could watch it from here."

She shook her head. "I not supposed to see this day

dawn. One sunrise begs another and another. I need to go before sun rises. I need to go now." She turned then and took her first steps into the cave, gingerly at first but then with more determination. Then she looked back. "You know that song?"

"Which song?"

She smiled at him and he noticed that colors were brightening behind her. The aurora borealis. "I remember I hear Elvis for first time. They play his songs at café in village. My mother, of course, she don't like it. First one I hear is 'Don't Be Cruel'. You know that song?"

"Yes I know it." His voice was hoarse.

"Sing it then." She closed her eyes and sang in a surprisingly strong voice. "You know I can be found, sitting home all alone—"."

Reginald joined in. "If you can't come around, at least please telephone. Don't be cruel, to whose heart is true—"

"Keep singing!" she called, waved one final time and walked into deeper into the cave. The light was stronger now, silver and rich colors. She was bathed in light, Lucia with her thick winter coat and huge boots. His eyes ached with it.

"Please let's forget the past, the future looks bright ahead—" Reginald kept singing as Lucia merged with the rainbow light. She turned one last time to look at him. It was hard to tell, she was so bright and beautiful, but he thought she mouthed 'keep singing'. All of the sudden there was a brilliant flash of light and Lucia and all the colors were gone.

"I don't want no other love, baby it's just you I'm thinking of." Reginald's voice trailed off and he felt something under his hand—Sparky's fluffy head. He patted him. "She's gone now, Sparks. Do you want to stay with me?"

Suddenly Sparky started barking, short, clipped barks and he started digging. He took something in his mouth and handed it to Reginald.

It was a tiny skull. Reginald turned it around in his hands like an elephant would do.

"Do you think its Colin's?" he asked the dog.

The dog cocked his head but didn't answer.

"I hope it is." Reginald looked at the sky, at the Matterhorn. "I hope he made it to the other other side too and is finally meeting his mother. He will be very proud of her." Reginald smiled, not noticing his own tears. Suddenly he was distracted by a light overhead. He looked up in time to see a shooting star streak across the sky. He held his breath. In the next heartbeat came another. Then another. They came faster and faster, filling the whole sky with light. Then they dwindled off and darkness settled over the sky again. He laid the tiny skull down.

"Come on Spark, let's go home." He walked away, whistling Don't Be Cruel under his breath. Sparky leapt and bounded beside him. When they were halfway down the mountain, the sun came up, setting the Matterhorn alight for a new day.

Chapter 18

Emma had smuggled an itchy green wool blanket from the basement (Zach had mused what other wonders were stored down there—fireworks, old military blankets, what else?) and they had been snuggled up like litter mates in an oversize lounge chair, watching the sky. The star canopy was incredible, there was none of the light pollution like back home that stole away the night. The blanket was amazing, it had kept them warm even though their breath froze as soon as it left their mouths and fell back on their faces in sprinkles. It was well after midnight, time for romance or bed, or both. But for Zach it was confession time, the moment of truth. His stomach roiled and he bit back a sour belch.

"I killed someone."

The words cut the frozen air and Emma stiffened in his arms.

"What? I'm sorry, I didn't understand you. I don't think my English is very good."

"No, I think you understood me correctly. Emma, I killed someone." He turned to look at her, her cheeks the color of freshly fallen snow an hour before dawn. "There is one less person on the earth because of me. She never will watch The Golden Girls again. Never sip a chocolate milkshake, never get a chance to play another round of bingo or click her dentures or go to an all-you-can-eat buffet or take a cruise. "

"What happened?" Emma asked.

He told the story in bursts, his gaze shifting from one star to the next as he talked. But he wasn't actually seeing the stars. He was back in the car with Anson. He didn't want to look at the horror or disappointment dawning in her eyes. At the end she took his hand that was lying on the wool blanket, weaving her fingers in with his. He twitched, wincing as if she had touched something tender. He hadn't been expecting that.

"You have a very heavy burden to carry."

"That's the understatement of the year." He looked back towards the hotel. He couldn't help it. His eyes were tearing up.

She squeezed his hand. "Look."

Streaks of light were racing across the sky.

"They are called Sternenkinder."

"What?"

She cuddled closer to him. "In German. They are called Sternenkinder. Star children, I guess you would translate it. The ones that never breathe earthly air. The ones that die before they are born. It is said that you can wish on them. Would you wish her memory away?"

"What?"

"The woman you killed. You would wish that away?"

Zach squeezed his eyes closed and pinched the bridge of his nose. "Yes. I wish it had never happened."

"Of course you do. But her memory, I mean. Would you rather forget all about her?"

He sighed. "No, I kind of, like, owe it to her. I can't really explain. The very least thing I can do for her is to think about her."

Emma squeezed his hand. "You didn't mean to kill her. It was an accident."

"That doesn't make any difference to her. She's dead."

"You said it, she's dead. But you are letting this destroy your life. If you don't recover from this, you will be as dead as she."

"But I killed her! You don't get it, I killed someone!" He inhaled sharply. "Sometimes my hands feel wet, you know? When I think about my mom's ugly sweater or what's for dinner or the next college basketball championship, I forget for a second, you see. Then my hands feel wet. It's her blood, reminding me of what I've done." He unraveled his fingers from hers and wiped them on the blanket. "It's like a stone in my belly with maggots crawling over it, it wobbles every time I move, reminding me. I have wet hands and a heavy stomach, every hour of every day of my life. I don't deserve to be alive and she is not!"

"Who chooses, who picks? Who decides who is more deserving of life?"

"Well I know for damn sure it shouldn't be me."

"What was her name?" Emma asked. "The lady who died."

"Mrs. Givens. Mrs. Hope Givens."

"Hope Givens? That was really her name?"

Zachary let out a pent-up breath. "Yes. Yes it was."

"Well if that isn't a sign, I don't know what is. Do you think she would forgive you? Mrs. Hope Givens?"

"I – I don't know! How should I know that?"

Emma squeezed his hand. "But the hardest thing to do is forgive yourself, isn't it?"

The sky fell down all around them.

Chapter 19

Reginald was in the dining room, staring out the window and not thinking much of anything. He supposed he was in a state of shock. He looked over when Cleona walked in, her dark purple aura wrapped around her like a cloak.

"Where have you been?" She slid into the seat across from him, and something under the table yelped. "Sparky! What are you doing here?" She reached down to pet him. Just yesterday she had told him he was her father. He noticed the rainbows danced in her jet black hair as if from a distance. "You didn't sleep in your room yesterday. You don't look so rested. Long night last night?"

She surprised a grin out of him. "Which are you trying to be— my daughter or my mother?"

She pitched a nervous giggle which sounded odd in her own ears. She wasn't accustomed to being nervous or to giggling. "Sorry, I didn't mean to sound controlling. I have no idea what to call you—Dad or Pops or Father?"

"Have you ever called anyone Dad?" Reginald replaced his coffee cup.

"Yes." She looked down at her fingers twirling nervously amongst themselves. "There was a man in California who I lived with and whom I called 'Dad' in the same way I used to call his wife 'Mom'. They adopted me, and they were good to me. At least as good as they were able to be. I never went to bed hungry unless I did something really terrible."

"That's good to know." He took a swallow of coffee. "You know, I almost got married. I was engaged when I was deployed to Vietnam. My fiancée was killed in a car accident while I was away. I felt guilty about that, I was the one who taught her to drive. I remained alone after she died, probably to punish myself. That was only that one time in Vietnam that I was with a woman. And then there was Lucia. I think I loved her from the moment I saw her picture on the internet. I just didn't realize it."

"Were you with Lucia last night? Is that why Sparky's with you?"

A sip of coffee came dribbling out of Reginald's mouth in a half-choke. He blotted the wayward drops up from the white tablecloth with a napkin. "Yes I was."

"How is she doing?"

Reginald blinked back the tears that threatened to spurt out. Oh no you don't, he thought. How was he going to explain Lucia's suicide to Cleona? He could still smell Lucia in wafts of spice and lavender. "She's happy, I think."

"I was kind of surprised to find you here. I thought you would be with her?"

Me too, he thought and a lungful of air hitched in his throat. My eyelids are a brick wall, my eyelids are a brick wall. "I think she needs some time alone just now. I'll catch up with her later." I'm sure I will, he thought. "And you? I thought you would be dissecting your meteorite by now?"

"I send it off by mail to the lab in Maryland this morning."

"You did?"

She levelled her gaze at him. "Suddenly it wasn't so important anymore. Looking back, I can't believe that I resorted to bribery and robbery to get ahold of it. I was searching for it for so long, but I was looking for the wrong thing. I was actually searching for you."

"I'm so sorry Cleona." He placed the spoon next to the cup. What would Private Miller want him to say? The voice from the grave was silent, so he had to improvise. Christ, he was so bad at people-ing. "I have to tell you something, but I don't know how."

Cleona folded her arms. "I guess you better just tell me then."

Reginald leaned forward, pinning Cleona with his blue eyes, eyes that matched hers. "I got confused for a while, you see. It all fit so perfectly. I was in Vietnam, you were born in Vietnam. I had an affair while I was in Vietnam. The dates match. Everything fits. Except its not true." He took a deep breath. "I am not your father, Cleona. I am not the one you are looking for."

She shook her head and her black hair fanned out. "I know its a lot for you to accept, but I'm not angry and I don't want any money from you. You don't have to deny it."

Reginald pounded the table with his fist, startling them both. "That's not it, Doctor Skye. You don't know how much I actually wished for it to be true! I would love a daughter, especially one as brilliant and talented as you! But you aren't my daughter."

"But the crystal? It fits perfectly together. Two halves make a whole. Unlike a fake meteorite, that would be difficult to stage."

"Oh its not staged. But its not my crystal. At least it wasn't always. It was given to me in Vietnam. And I guess the man who gave it to me—he would be your father."

"Not you?"

"No."

Cleona cleared her throat, but then she nodded, seeming to accept this. Only her aura darkened. "But then you knew him, my father?"

"Yes. He was a soldier in the company I was commanding."

"Do you know where he is now?"

"He's dead, dear Cleona. I am so so sorry."

Cleona squeezed her eyes shut. Her aura went from dark violet to black. A whirlwind of pity and guilt raged inside Reginald. He reached out and took her hand.

"I was so sure," she said. "Everything fit perfectly, like you said. Like the two halves of the crystal." She opened her eyes, "Are you positive?"

"Yes. But I do wish it were different. I even thought about not telling you, for selfish and selfless reasons, but a woman like you thrives on the truth, on facts."

"You're right about that." She managed a small grin.

"But I'll make you an offer. I'm not your father. I didn't earn that privilige. And I won't ask you to pretend that I am. That would dishonor the memory of your real father. But perhaps, for a bit, you can treat me as though I were."

"What do you mean?"

"I guess I want to hear about your first time riding a bicycle, the first tooth you lost, your first boyfriend. All the pieces that comprise your life."

Cleona grinned. Her black aura turned back into purple. "I tried to screw my tooth back in, the first one I lost. What a bloody mess!"

"I can't wait to hear all your stories." Reginald answered her grin with a rueful one of his own. "But unfortunately we don't have much time to do it." He looked out the window. Snowflakes were dancing like diamonds in the sun. There wasn't a cloud to be seen. Homeless snowflakes.

"Diamond dust."

"What?"

"Snowflakes falling from a clear sky. The colloquial term is 'diamond dust'."

"Cleona, I have to tell you something else." Reginald leaned forward. "I have brain cancer. I was diagnosed just before I came here. It was actually the reason for my trip. Something to cross off my bucket list, because that particular pail is approaching fast. Motoring along and gaining speed. I saw a picture of Lucia on the Internet and I was searching for the ghost of my own father, and well, a lot of other things fell in place and that's why I'm here."

Cleona laid the butter knife down like a surgical instrument that she had just discovered was useless. "Are you serious? How long do you have to live?"

He looked at her helplessly. Just then the voice from the grave piped up. "It is she that will find you," Private Miller had said. "Less than a year."

He had shouted at Private Miller when his boots were incorrectly laced. He had yanked Private Miller from the respite of sleep and marched him into a foreign jungle, forcing him to walk in front. He might as well, have pushed Private Miller from a cliff, pointed a loaded gun at his head, tightened the noose around his skinny neck. In spite of all that, Private Jacob Miller had turned around and did the most amazing thing. Private Miller gave Reginald, at a point in his life when he had nothing else to look forward to except death, the chance to matter to someone.

"Have you ever loved?" Lucia had asked. Yes, he had. Now, he had.

"I'll try to be the best father figure that I can for as long as I can. You deserve better, Cleona, but this—" he patted his heart,—"is all I can give you."

Cleona took his hand across the table. "It will be enough."

They held hands in the room splashed by light and color.

"Do you have a husband?"

"No. There is a guy—" she broke off. "No. I'm not married."

"Children? Pets?"

"No, I'm alone."

"Well, if you don't have anyone waiting for you or any pressing plans, why don't you stay with me in Zermatt for a while?"

"At this hotel? I can't afford it."

"I know a place where we can stay. Are you up for an adventure?"

She beamed and her aura turned lavender and silver. "Always!"

"Good. Put on your snow pants and walking boots. I'll explain on the way." Sparky snuck out from under the table and barked his approval. "And I'll tell you everything that I remember about your father. And my memory happens to be quite good."

Chapter 20

Amanda stood at the head of the hotel driveway, squinting in the morning sun. The Leaning Tower of Luggage was piled up beside her. She had already checked out with Claudia (trying to keep her expression neutral while looking at the gigantic bill) and bid her farewell.

The sliding doors behind her rolled open.

Zach was carrying his snowboard under one arm and his suitcase was clunking behind him. "I never even got to use it." He propped the snowboard up against the wall beside the door.

"Maybe your father will take you next year—somewhere a bit closer to home," she said. She started to wipe her itching eye but caught herself in time. Her infection was starting to get improve, and she didn't want risk irritating it again.

"I'm not sure I want to take any more trips with him. Nothing can top the time I had with you."

Amanda laughed. "I'm sure. But you are young and lots of adventures await you. And your father should be so lucky as to get to spend time with you. He should be so lucky." Spontaneously she hugged him, and he did not pull away. He felt strong in her arms, like hugging a sun-warmed tree. "I am so proud of you, Zach."

"Thanks for everything, Mom. You had to put up with a lot of my b.s. this year. I'm really sorry about that." His chest hitched under her cheek and she stepped back. He was a little taller than she was and he had unfinished business with growth hormones. Soon he would be rocketing skyward, going to college, maybe getting married one day.

"You don't have to apologize honey. That's what moms do."

"Yes I do have to apologize!" He met her gaze. "I can't thank you enough for sticking by me. I was a complete dick to you and you didn't deserve that."

"Sit on your language, don't forget." She grinned. "Apology accepted, then."

"Emma told me that the hardest thing to do was to forgive myself. She's right about that, but I'm going to try."

"That girl is wise beyond her years. Did you say goodbye to her already?"

"Yeah but it was hard. I mean we can always Facetime but it's not the same, you know."

Amanda knew. She didn't mention that it would be a long time before Zach saw Emma again, if ever. But who could say? It was easier than ever for star-crossed lovers to stay in touch, who was she to write them off?

Stranger things had happened.

"Maybe you should start by apologizing to yourself. You've been a dick to yourself too."

"Sit on your language." He pointed down the street. "Is that our ride?"

A limousine pulled up to the door, as sleek as wet leather.

Amanda laughed. "I'm afraid not."

The sliding doors swished open again and Vera

emerged like a hibernating bear out of a cave, wearing an orange tunika the size of a four-man tent, silver bracelets clanking on her wrists.

"Can I help you with your luggage, Ma'am?" Zach asked.

Vera blinked, startled. "No thank you. The driver can manage, I'm sure."

An energy rose up in Amanda. Before she had a chance to think, she reached out and took Vera's elbow. "Can I ask you something, ma'am?"

Vera blinked again and her tiny mouth rounded in a smile, her teeth miniature pearls. "Of course, dear."

"Are you all right?"

"Why do you ask, pet?"

"Well, you are always by yourself and sometimes, well, it seems like you are talking to yourself."

Vera laughed. "Why, I am talking to myself! I am the best conversationalist that I know!"

"What are you talking to yourself about?" Zachary asked.

"Well, young sir, there is no mystery about that! I enjoy counting my blessings. I do that every time I come here. This week I was discussing the ways to make wishes."

"What?" Mother and son asked in unison.

"Wishes! There are so many things to make wishes on—chicken's wishbones, a wayward eyelash, a found penny, a coin tossed in a fountain, dandelions, license plates with three numbers in a row, a genie's lamp. So many things to be wished upon—"

"And shooting stars." Zachary said. "Don't forget about shooting stars."

Vera laughed again. "Oh my dear boy. You aren't supposed to wish on falling stars. You are supposed to put them back in the sky. That's what they are made for. You know, there are lots of ways to erase things and start over. You can erase things on a blackboard, you can erase what you write in pencil. Meteorites have been the great erasers on earth, sometimes wiping everything out for a fresh start. And everyone needs a fresh start sometimes, a clean slate, a second chance. To be a good parent, to be a good child, to find love. To forget and to remember. It's never too late. Hope forgives you, you know. Hope always gives you a second chance. I wish you all the luck in the world." She blew them a kiss and bundled herself into the limo. The driver somehow managed to load her seven suitcases into the trunk and whisked her away.

Zach scratched his head. "How did she know all those things, Mom?"

"She was always listening, wasn't she? And even when you fall down, for one second you are flying."

"Mom, are you feeling all right?"

Amanda gave his arm a squeeze. Yes, sometimes you had to fall to find yourself. To forgive yourself. To get your second chance. "I'm just fine, honey. For the first time in a while. I'm ready to go home. Let's call a taxi, shall we?"